THE HENRYVILLE 7

PALMETTO
PUBLISHING
Charleston, SC
www.PalmettoPublishing.com

Paperback ISBN: 979-8-8229-3431-3

THE HENRYVILLE 7

BASED ON TRUE EVENTS

By: Robert Woody

CONTENTS

Snapshot: *Shockoe Bottoms Slave Depot,*

Richmond, Virginia [1846] 5

The Two Trees 7

The Henryville Seven 13

The Trial 23

Snapshot: *Inner City Blues,*

The Adventures of Corey Colson 33

Present Day: *Norfolk, Virginia* 38

Snapshot 46

Snapshot: *Skid Row, Los Angeles* 50

Richmond, Virginia: *(2 Weeks Later)* 53

Snapshot: *Mughali Abasi Mosque, Chicago, Illinois* 66

Richmond, Va. 70

Snapshop: *Inner City Blues,*

The Adventures of Corey Colson 74

Snapshot: *Prestone, Alabama* 84

The Baltimore Star Newspaper: *Baltimore, Maryland* 91

Richmond, Virginia 137

Robert Eugene Woody

Teaching professional with proven experience in physical education, recreation and other related fields.

Date of birth: December 27, 1955

1985

420 Courtland St. N.E.
Atlanta, GA 30308
404-399-2855
Email: woodyrob05@gmail.com

EDUCATION:

B. S. in Physical Education
The University of Maryland Eastern Shore
(Princess Anne, MD) (1979)

EXPERIENCE:

Teacher / Coach in the school systems that include:

- Intramural Sports Director University of Maryland Eastern Shore (Princess Anne, MD) (1980–1982)
- Athletic Director, Peg Leg Bates Country Club (Kerhonkson, NY) (1983)
- Wake County Schools (Raleigh, NC) (1983–1986, 1997–1998)
- Baltimore City Schools (Baltimore, MD) (1987–1988)
- Atlanta Parks and Recreation (1988)
- Martinsville City Schools (Martinsville, VA) (1992–1994)
- Los Angeles USD (Santa Monica, CA) (1995–1997)
- Game Day Operations Atlanta Braves (Atlanta, GA) (2000)
- Roofing Contractor (Norfolk, VA), (Atlanta, GA)(2001–Present)
- Roof and Gutter Repairs, Precision Services (Atlanta, GA) (2016–Present)

AWARDS:

- Most Valuable Player in football Fieldale—Collinsville High School (Collinsville, VA) (1973)
- Letterman's Award in Tennis UMES (Princess Anne, MD) (1979)
- United States Air Force ROTC Academic Scholarship (1975)

EXTRA CURRICULAR ACTIVITIES:

- Tennis Instructor
- Bowling
- Basketball Referee (youth, league & high school)
- Alpha Phi Alpha Fraternity Inc (AΦA)

Present

956 Lawton St, SW

Atlanta, GA 30310

Snapshot

Shockoe Bottoms Slave Depot
Richmond, Virginia [1846]

Edow, shackled and hungry, walked slowly up the gang plank to the large open arena. His entire village was overrun by members of the Ashanti tribesmen with the help of 12 musket armed English slave traders. For 4 days the captives were herded through dense jungle terrain to the awaiting slave ships along the slave Coast of Africa. There were over 300 men, women and children stuffed into the damp and crowded bowels of the ship. The group was led through a large gauntlet of slave brokers and plantation owners, eager to bid on the next crop of human pillage.

After being corralled into an 8 foot deep observation pit, pit boss Hayden Lloyd cracked his bullwhip and the opening bell was rung to bring the auction to order. Hayden was well compensated to keep the festivities moving briskly. Armed guards were strategically stationed to deter any attempts to escape. Slave traders and potential owners were also closely watched because forged paperwork and other vises had crept into the depot by unscrupulous brokers trying to cash in on any advantage they could muster.

Three armed guards stepped to the front of the stage and fired their muskets to further settle down the crowd, signaling the start of the auction.

"Now that I have your attention, we will now let these people know what the consequences will be if any of you try to escape." Hayden pointed to the big curtain on his left and they slowly began to open. A stark naked Negro slave was hung by his neck, with large welts of torn skin all over his body. Then he violently flecked his bullwhip and a large watermelon that was sitting on a guidepost shattered. The slaves were terrified with fear. The message was clear.

This scene is repeated 2 to 4 times a day to whet the appetite for cheap labor across this suddenly prosperous new nation. Shockoe Bottoms has cemented itself as the northernmost gateway for slave labor for the middle and upper states. Banks and insurers profited considerably to see that this most precious human cargo reached its appropriate destination. This launched the country's first millionairs and established Richmond, Virginia as a major player in the lucrative slave trade.

2

The Two Trees

"Here come momma and daaadeeee!" Emphasis is on daddy.

Never venture out of hearing distance when Diane and Lee Woods got home from work. You could see their car slowly creeping behind the caravan of cars heading home at least a mile away. The problem was, if you are on punishment, you had better be in the yard when they pulled into the driveway. Love hurts, if you get my meaning.

Baldy jumped straight up from his dice game and sprinted for home. It was his turn to light out for home. Over a fence he leaped, ignoring the briar patches and low flying limbs that instantly reminded him what to look forward to if he didn't beat his folks back home. Baldy was tossing a deflated football into the air as Diane and Lee pulled into the driveway.

"Man, just in time!" Baldy had done all of his chores, but that still would not have been enough to save him from a whipping if he wasn't there.

In the summer of 1958, Martin County, in rural southwest Virginia, was a typical hotbed for segregation, hangings and racial hatred spewed in the direction of most colored people. Most of the time they were referred to as niggers or coons, which usually sparked up some kind of confrontation that left a colored man dead and a white one vindicated. You could go Into Caney's Restaurant to order a sandwich or a meal, but colored people had to wait for their food around back. The food would careen down a chute and slam into a door. If the door was broken, everything ended up in the dirt.

Robert "Baldy" Woods grew up just outside of Henryville in Martin County, just off Fig Road. It was a small house on the top of a hill overlooking the major thoroughfare for commuters to and from work into town. The children in the neighborhood were constantly bussed to the far reaches of the county to satisfy hastily mandated segregation laws. Baldy was constantly in trouble; picking fights with white students, stealing and breaking bus windows. He was kind of small in stature, so he was often on the short end of a skirmish. He also paid dearly when he got home. Every misdeed was accompanied by a letter to his parents, doubling the punishment.

Lee Woods fought hard to keep his son in school. He didn't want him to grow up working in one of the local furniture factories for low pay or promotions. He wanted better for his only son.

One day at the Sunday morning breakfast table, Lee caught his son off guard by asking him what he wanted to be when he grew up.

"A convict!" Baldy said proudly.

Lee spat his food out all over the table. He couldn't respond.

"Boy, you are so stupid!" Lena and her younger sister snickered at their older brother.

Baldy didn't understand. Colored convicts were constantly working the roadways, so he thought it was the only jobs for black people.

His mother gave him a quick explanation of what a convict was and Baldy realized he had let his father down again.

The exchange left Baldy feeling sad because he badly wanted to please his father. So he tried to do better in school. He stopped fighting in school and started making better grades. Things were starting to look up. That is, until the kids in the neighborhood came up with a very new and risky past-time.

Rocking cars.

The older kids in the neighborhood would stand behind the two trees, a local gathering spot next to Baldy's house, and wait until a car or truck got almost directly underneath. Suddenly, a torrent of gravel would rain down, forcing the irate traveler to slam on the breaks. But by the time they turned around, the guilty party had retreated to their house or a hiding place to watch. Some of the bolder ones would change clothes and walk right back by their victims as they spewed their hatred and contempt to a local sheriff's deputy.

"Got damn niggers! Can't you do something about this shit deputy? That's the second time they done hit my car. The last time they broke my window plumb out!" Edgar Caney was on his way back to his daddy's store and restaurant. He talked rudely to any black people that came into the store. Every kid that went there tried to steal candy or anything else they could get in their pockets. He was also on the losing end of many of the fights that broke out at Henry High School because of his attitude.

Strolling back past the scene was Freddie Dean and Michael Watkins. Freddie had changed into a white t-shirt, sunglasses and a big beige sombrero. Michael sported flip-flops and dirty bib overalls. Baldy had seen the pair sprinting by and already knew what had happened.

"Is this the boy that threw the rocks?" Deputy Blain Parsons couldn't catch the boys either. From the vicinity of the two trees that hovered over the highway, there was ample cover to launch their missiles without being seen.

"Hell naw, they were older! But I seen'm. But you can take this little nigger to jail anyway. Shit, he does it too."

"Hell Edgar, I can't do that. This ain't nothin' but a kid."

"Got dammit, its kids that's doin' it! Take'm all to jail. I don't give a fuck. And you know what Blain, when I tell my daddy that I called you and you didn't arrest somebody, you might be lookin' for another job."

Baldy was beginning to get nervous. Things were working out quite well at home since his change of attitude. He had to think of something quick.

"I ain't been out of this yard all day! And Edgar Caney, you know my daddy. If you tell this lie on me and he found out you said it, he ain't gonna care who your daddy is. And you know that."

Freddie and Michael walked up.

"Ya'll messin' with Mr. Woods' kid? Man, he ain't gone like that." Freddie Dean to the rescue. Any trouble in the neighborhood would eventually end up on Freddie's or Michael's doorstep. All of the kids learned the proper art of rocking cars from them.

Edgar Caney thought not very long about that.

"Well, ... ah, if any of you niggers get caught throwing rocks, you gonna pay!" Edgar dejectedly walked to his car and left.

Baldy was good for another day.

Most of the children on Fig Road had a nickname. Robert Woods (Baldy) got his because his dad took him to the barber shop every week. His best friend was Duane "Hamburger" Williams. Hamburger was big for his age and never turned down a chance to eat. Because of his size, he was a good one to have around when trouble started. Al "Tree" Samuels, a gangly soul who lived next door to Baldy, stood a good 3 to 4 inches above the rest of the kids in the neighborhood.

Summer was slowly drawing to a close and school and bus assignments were beginning to appear. Instead of providing better equipment and facilities for the Negro teachers and students, most of their schools were closed and everyone was transferred to white schools across the county and city. School administrators were ill equipped to handle the logistical and disciplinary nightmare that was bound to be unleashed.

Fights and suspicions ensued, with Colored students taking the brunt of the negative consequences that followed. White students that were receptive of the changes were soon marginalized. There were no remedies acceptable for either side.

Most students were productive in their segregated environments. In the colored and white schools, discipline was a respected and necessary vehicle to drive home the rules of the law. But white parents openly pushed the notion that "... a nigger teacher will not put your hand on my child!" Therefore, corporal punishment was outlawed in virtually every instance, stripping teachers of control of the classroom, and turned administrators (principals and guidance counselors) into political lightweights. This gave extremists on both sides of the aisle free rein to pursue their agenda. Utter chaos ensued. Not only did the ruling handicap the schools, the legislation prevented parents from touching their own children. Drug use and criminal activity became rampant in both city and county schools. It set into motion, race baiting, dumbed down academic requirements, and a generally negligent attitude about most contacts between races; except one.

The mixing of races.

There was no way to anticipate the clandestine rendezvous of teenage white girls and black boys before, during and after school. Many tales of narrow escape from the second floor, windows and back doors, saved many black boys from a terrible fate.

Dating and marrying in Virginia was illegal. When Negro men got caught, the strange fruit hanging from a large tree in their neighborhood is usually a stark reminder to "… know your place!" With the integration of schools, it cranked up the pressure.

The Henryville Seven

Deborah Caney was intrigued by her new classmates. "Jungle Fever", white girls secretly dating Negro men, quickly spread like a wildfire. Drug and alchohol parties were held frequently at Freddie Dean's house. Freddie was a high school dropout who blamed all of his shortcomings on something or somebody else. Michael Watkins was his flunky, always agreeing with everything Freddie said or did. The two were inseparable.

At least once a month, Freddie and Michael brought their conquests back to Freddie's little bungalow late at night out of sight of the neighbors. The girls would be vanquished well before sunup because if his dad had an idea of what was going on, even slick talking Freddie couldn't get out of that.

It was the last Sunday before school started, so they wanted to get the new year off with a party. The guys had arranged quite a reception for Deborah Caney. They both got caught stealing from her father's store. This was their chance to get even.

The moon shone brightly in the starry sky as Michael tapped on Danny Mann's door. Danny is about 6 eggs short of a dozen and had fewer teeth than Popeye the Sailor. They were joined by Floyd Jenkins and Richard Hairston, older men in the neighborhood. Filled to the rim with some of the best bootleg from Franklin County and puffing on a phat joint of weed, they boastfully prepped themselves for a fun night out. The two trees was the perfect place to steel their nerves for the party.

Al, Baldy and Duane read comic books and talked about the upcoming school year on Baldy's porch. Michael and his band of merry men were getting louder as the time got near.

"Man, they sure are loud. Lets go see what they doing." Duane was always admiring the antics of Michael and Freddie. He also got to stay out a little bit later because his father worked the second shift at the local furniture factory. He was definitely a mama's boy.

"I don't know fellas. If I go back in the house smelling like weed and alchohol, I'll have to start this year off like the last; with a sore ass." Baldy pointed to his backside and everybody laughed.

Al was a couple of years younger and always shied away from the older guys. "Count me out. I'm going home." He stood up and started for home next door.

"Come on Baldy. We got a little bit of time. Lets go see what they doin'."

"Ok. Just for a minute. Daddy will come looking for me if I ain't out here."

The pair walked over to the two trees and were immediately pulled into the group. "Look at this shit. Ain't you boys out past your bedtime?" Michael always gave the boys a bad time. "Hey Hamburger, you wanna hit this?" Richard held out a joint and Duane took a long, deep drag and began to cough.

"That's my boy! Now Baldy, your turn." Baldy didn't want to, but he would have been run off. It wasn't the first time for him to smoke weed, but it was the first time with these guys. He took a deep drag and held it. He held up fine.

Michael looked down at his watch. "Fellas, we got to get a move on. We gonna be late for the party." He put his arms around Hamburger and Baldy. "Hey, you boys want to go to a party? There's beer and a little surprise for ya. How about it?"

Duane's eyes were big and red from the weed. He didn't hesitate to pipe in, "Yeah, I'll go!"

"Well Baldy, what about you? Can you hang?"

"No way! School starts tomorrow. Hamburger, I'll see ya later." Baldy walked towards home.

****

"Oh Freddie, if my daddy knew I was here he would pitch a bitch straight to hell." Deborah Caney was naked and smelled of hot sex. "Give me something to drink baby."

Freddie looked at her with disgust. "Sure baby. Here's some boot with a beer chaser. Have at it." Deborah swallowed deeply and the concoction went down smoothly. Her head began to swim and she slowly laid back on the bed.

Michael tapped lightly on the kitchen window and then opened the front door. Freddie's eyes widened as he ushered in the motley crew. As Duane stepped in, Freddie stuck out his hand.

"Whoa, what is this? What is this kid doing here?"

"Don't worry about it Freddie. I told Hamburger he could come along. He can wait in the kitchen until we finish. Let him get something to eat. He may want to take a turn in the back, if you get my drift." Michael blinked his right eye and Freddie smiled.

"Ok."

****

Martin County High School always started each school year the same way. Deputy sheriffs were stationed strategically inside and outside the school to quell fights and mischief. For some reason there seemed to be a lot more deputies checking each bus as it pulled in front of the school. As bus #897 arrived, Baldy, Al and Hamburger shuffled from the back. Two deputies were on each side of the bus door.

"Show me your class schedule," was the greeting Deputy Coby Bassnight gave each student as he or she left the bus. Principal Jason Hooker watched intently as the bus began to empty.

"I wonder whats goin' on?" Baldy whispered to Hamburger. "They didn't even check any of the girls stuff."

"Ah, they just tryin' to scare everybody. They don't want us here anyway." Hamburger said it loud enough for the whole bus to hear.

Baldy, then Al stepped off the bus and their schedule was checked. Hamburger pulled his crumpled schedule out of his back pocket and handed it to Deputy Bassnight. He unfolded the paper and gazed wide-eyed at Hamburger.

"This is one of them!" he shouted. Two gigantic deputy sheriffs slammed Hamburger to the sidewalk face first. Blood spurted from his nose and right ear.

"What are you doing ? What did I do?" Two of hamburger's teeth laid on the sidewalk as he slowly began to black out. Pandemonium ensued as the masses began to pummel each other. Al and Baldy got caught up in the melee, fist and feet flying in all directions. Danny Mann slipped out the back of the bus unnoticed. He ran through the parking lot and into the woods.

Police and ambulance sirens screamed as teachers began to weave into the fracas. The only black teachers at Martin High School, Mrs. Bradshaw, a math teacher, and Mr. Holley, the boy's basketball coach, were also attacked. Coach Holley fought off a few undersized students and whisked Mrs. Bradshaw inside the front entrance.

Hamburger was carried unconscious to a police car and driven away. Additional deputies arrived with batons in hand and several dogs to restore order. Al straddled a white student on the front lawn, wildly striking where he could find an opening. Baldy ran over to pull him off. He couldn't believe what he was seeing. Al was always easy going.

"Al, let him go! You'll kill him!"

"Call me a nigger again faggot, and I will beat your ass into next week!" The boy couldn't respond; he was out cold.

All of the Negro students were herded into the school auditorium, about 150 total. The white students were sent to their homerooms, but were not allowed to attend any classes. Several kids of both races simply left the school grounds to walk or drive home.

Principal Hooker and Vice-Principal Gilbert walked onstage to address the students. The school nurse and several older students walked through the crowd bandaging wounds in various degrees of severity and consoling the rest. Sheriffs deputies slowly filed in and took up positions in the aisles and both entrances.

Jesse Toliver, a senior on the football team stood up.

"What ya'll doin' attacking us like that?" We ain't gonna take this shit all year! We gonna fight back!"

A collective "hell yeah" and "damn right" went through the crowd. They were restless and they wanted answers now. Anxious deputies inched in at the ready.

Mr. Gilbert stepped to the podium on stage. "Please people settle down. Everybody get a seat. Look, we'll get ya'll up to speed and send ya'll back home for the day. Officer Bassnight will make a quick statement and you can get out of here."

The auditorium grew gradually quiet as Bassnight stepped forward.

"First of all, I'm real sorry for all this stuff going on this morning, but we got a real serious problem here. Last night a young lady was brutally raped and assaulted. She was dropped off in the parking lot of her father's store and left for dead. The family dog did attack one of the men and took a big gash out of his leg. We found the dog with a piece of his pants leg still in his mouth.

"The girl's parents got up from all the barking and found her outside and took her to county hospital. She identified 7 men and boys that took part in raping her. We rounded everybody up but one juvenile and we are looking for him now. We also arrested a young boy in front of the school this morning."

Baldy was stunned. Hamburger was his usual boisterous self and didn't mention anything about that. Besides, Hamburger was probably still a virgin and wouldn't dream of such a thing.

****

Danny Mann slithered over fences and through back yards to no place in particular. He walked and ran briskly, weaving in and out of the woods towards home. He had taken his turn in Freddie's back room with Deborah Caney, but she laughed at him. Danny slapped her, bringing an abrupt end to the party.

Peeping in both directions, Danny finally eased out unto Fig Road and the final few hundred yards to his parent's mobile home. One quick check and he sprinted to the back door and hurried in. The whole trailer shook as he violently slammed the door.

He thought he was safe.

Deputy Jason Patrick motioned for the two officers to cover the back door. They crept stealthly from behind the trees and leaned against the trailer to listen for any movement. Several others abandoned their vehicles and brandished shotguns, rifles and sidearms.

Patrick surveyed his men and pointed two fingers at the front door. "Boom, boom, boom" was fist on door. "Danny Mann! Sheriff's Department! Open the door now!"

Danny ran into the back room and reached into the bedroom closet. He grabbed a gas can and matches, frantically piling up clothes in the front hallway. After dousing the clothes, he trailed the gas back to his room and set it on fire. Flames raced down the hallway and quickly engulfed the front rooms. He closed the door and locked it.

Smoke billowed from every crevice, the intense heat violently blowing out the front windows.

"Kick them doors in!" Patrick yelled. "Get a firetruck out here now, got dammit!"

Firetrucks were on the scene in five minutes. With frantic precision, the fire was out in mere minutes.

"Danny, where are you?" Firemen poked and prodded through the rubble looking for any signs of life. When they got to the back bedroom, Danny was sprawled on the floor. He wasn't breathing.

The sirens wailed as they left for the hospital. Medics worked feverishly to bring Danny back. Finally, a faint pulse. He wasn't going to get off that easy.

****

Baldy went with Hamburger's parents to visit him at the Henryville Correctional Center. All seven defendants were housed in the single cell unit of the jail, pending trial. The Commonwealth Attorney's Office announced early on that Virginia law allowed them to seek the death penalty in a rape case that "... rips at the basic fabric of this law-abiding community." There would be no bond.

Hamburger was escorted into the small congregation area by two large jailers. Tears rolled down both sides of his face and leaped freely from his cheeks. His hands and feet were shackled, jingling with each step. Hamburger looked like only a frail outline of his former self. He had lost about 30 pounds in only a few months.

"Mama, daddy, I didn't do nothin'. I was just hangin' out with Michael and Freddie. I was in the kitchen eating."

Tears began to slowly trickle from Marla Williams eyes. She said nothing.

"They say ya'll raped that white girl and left her out there like trash. We brought you up better than that, Duane." George Williams was a slight, but stern man. He had argued constantly with his wife about the way she coddled and protected their son. There would be no mercy coming from him.

"Baldy, I didn't do nothin'! They was in the back room drinking and smoking weed. I didn't even know she was back there until we left. All I did was ride with'em to drop her off." Hamburger was wide-eyed and overwhelmed by the serious predicament he now faced.

"I know you ain't lyin' Hamburger. Just hang in there. Everything will come out at the trial. You'll see. You'll be out of here in no time!" Baldy didn't believe that himself. Old man Caney had stacked the deck. Word had quickly spread about the rape. It didn't look good for his daughter to be carrying on like this, because he was a Ku Klux Klan controlling officer.

"Times' up. You folks gotta leave."

It would be the last time Baldy saw Hamburger alive.

The Trial

The Martin County Courthouse was packed. Only the back two rows of the upper balcony were empty. Those seats were reserved for relatives of the accused. With a high profile case like this, it would be too dangerous for Negros to venture anywhere near the building.

Five men and two juveniles, which were charged as adults, are on trial for rape, attempted murder and assault. Laws and penal codes that had been on the books for many years were used to seek the death penalty. Freddie Dean, Michael Watkins, Floyd Jenkins, Richard Hairston and Jeffrey Harris, whose car Deborah Caney identified as the one used to transport her home and as the driver, were charged with rape and attempted murder. Duane Williams and Danny Mann, the minors, were charged with rape and assault.

The defendants would all be tried together and represented by the law firm Blue, Forrest and Frazier from Richmond, Virginia. They petitioned the court for a change of venue, but the motion was enthusiastically denied by Judge Alwin Agar, a fervent defender of segregation and no friend to Negros. His nickname was the "Prince of Pinstripes" because of the stiff sentences he handed out for minor offenses.

The prosecutor, Thandy Martin, was a direct descendant of the county's namesake and well connected. He, Edgar Caney Sr. and Judge Agar ran bootleg to the mountains of Tennessee as teenagers. They parlayed their little adventure into a lucrative furniture manufacturing business that set them up for life. Agar went to the University of Tennessee Law School. Martin tested the political waters and found out he had the gift of persuasion. Caney built a big restaurant that sold fresh produce and good meals out the front door and bootleg and sometimes deeds of evil out the back.

The spectators in the courtroom were loud and boisterous. Deputies strolled attentively down the aisles, looking for any sign of weapons. The entire trial will be broadcast live by the local radio station.

Reporters and photographers from around the state were crammed along the walls. About 100 locals had to wait outside for regular updates from their colleagues inside. A large Confederate flag flew menacing in the morning breeze. Pictures of Jefferson Davis, Robert E. Lee and Taylor Henry, the town's namesake, hung strategically behind the judge's chair.

Tension rose as at exactly 11:00am, Judge Alwin Agar swung open the chamber door and approached the bench. The entire courtroom stood and waited for him to take his seat. He was a giant figure, his teeth stained from the constant presence of the chewing tobacco in his custom made robe's pocket.

The bailiff strode up to the judge and whispered something inaudibly into his ear.

"Bam, bam, bam!" The judge slammed his gavel and the courtroom came to order.

"Now before I bring this here jury in, there are some things we need to get straight. First thing is I don't want you newspaper people running in and out of this courtroom. Ya'll find a spot and stay in it until we take a break. And bailiff, check them Caney's again for weapons because I don't want no trouble from Richmond while we do justice."

Two deputies checked all twelve of the Caneys and nodded to the judge.

"Alright, bring'em in."

The jurors, 12 local white men, filed into the courtroom. A loud roar came up as Jimmy Joyce, the 5th juror to enter, came into view. He doffed his cap and bowed to the courtroom. Laughter broke out as he missed his seat and slammed butt first to the floor.

"Bam, bam, bam!"

"Order, order! Ya'll this is serious business. I will kindly ask all of you to remember this or you might be spending a few days back yonder! Now, settle down."

"Now, bring in the prisoners."

The courtroom was hushed as the door swung open by a deputy. One by one, Freddie Dean, then Michael Watkins were followed by the rest of the defendants. Chains jangled from the hand restraints and leg irons that bound them. Hamburger had cried the entire time he was in jail. He anxiously scanned the room for his parents. They were not there.

Danford Blue would serve as the lead attorney for the defense and would be handling all of the examinations and crosses. It will be a daunting task for such a young and inexperienced lawyer.

After opening statements, Thandy Martin called his first witness.

"Your Honor, I would like to call to the stand Miss Deborah Caney." Thandy was firm and dramatic. The doors in the back of the courtroom swung open and Deborah Caney stepped inside. She wore a white dress with green and blue flowers on it. The dark sunglasses on her pale white face didn't hide the black and red bruises underneath. Red scratches covered her arms and legs as she purposely marched down the aisle and took her seat on the witness stand.

Wide-eyed gawkers covered their mouths and glared in horror as Deborah reached up and removed the glasses to reveal the tremendous beating she had suffered. A collective "Oh my God" could be heard as the blinding flashes of the cameras did their work. A monstrous black right eye, still healing, outraged everyone.

"Order! Order in this courtroom! Bailiff, clear this courtroom of the next person that makes a sound."

The courtroom grew quiet as Martin confidently walked towards the witness. The gruesome scene had its desired effect.

"Now ma'am, would you please tell the court your name."

Deborah Caney stared blankly at no one in particular. After a short pause, she said, "Deborah Marie Caney."

"And on August 21st of this year, what did you do?"

"Well, after church me and my sister Clara went over to our cousin Jenny Lee's house to look at some magazines and pick out some school clothes and talk."

"What happened when you left?"

"Me and Clara was gonna stay over for the night but I wanted to listen to my favorite radio program. The radio wasn't working so I decided to walk home."

"What happened when you left?"

"That's when I saw that Negra standing by the mailbox." Deborah pointed but never looked at the defense table.

"Well, which boy did you see, Miss Caney?"

"It, ... it was the one they call Freddie. Freddie Dean is his name."

"Did Mr. Dean say anything to you?"

"Yeah. He said, 'I got something I want you to give to your daddy for me.' And I said, 'What is it?' and then he said, 'Come here and I will show you.' So I went with him."

"And what did he do to you when you went inside?"

"I object, Your Honor!" Danford Blue's chair shot straight back as he stood. "The prosecution is leading the witness."

"Objection sustained. Rephrase counselor."

"Yes, Your Honor. What happened when you went inside Miss Caney?"

Deborah looked nervously at her father and brother on the front row. They glared back intently with an unforgiving scowl. Edgar Caney Sr.'s eyes narrowed and small red veins appeared. He was about to explode from his seat because of the agony this scene had dropped on his family.

Deborah stood up, and for the first time, she looked directly at Freddie Dean.

"That's when he took me! He raped me! Then he let them other men in and they raped me too and they beat me and kept on taking me. I didn't know what to do. I couldn't fight them off so I guess I just passed out." She slowly sat down in her seat and sobbed loudly.

"Girl, you lyin'! Ain't nobody ever had to take nothin' from you and you know it!" Sheriff's deputies quickly moved in to restrain Freddie.

Again the gallery got loud and started throwing anything they could get their hands on at the defense table.

"Kill them niggers!" A large group surged towards the defendants and they braced for the worst. That is, until two state troopers assigned to the courtroom stepped in between the groundswell and cocked their shotguns. Everyone stopped in their tracks and gingerly walked backwards.

"Bailiffs, clear this courtroom now. This trial is adjourned and will reconvene at 10:00 am."

Edgar Sr. grabbed his daughter by the arm and yanked her out of a side entrance and vanished. Edgar Jr. followed close behind, making sure nobody followed.

An uneasy calm came over Henryville that night. Claudette's Restaurant, in the white section of town, was loud, but guarded. Police were out in full force to see that nothing, or no one, got out of control.

The houses on Fig Road were quiet and alert. Every snap of a twig or barking dog tested nerves that were frayed and spent. This would be the longest night ever!

The courtroom was much more subdued the next day. Deputies executed full body searches of all the men at the door and state police were stationed strategically throughout. A long line formed early and national news organizations began to descend on this tiny enclave. In a surprising move, the prosecution rested, Thandy feeling the previous day's testimony would be enough to cement the case.

Deborah Caney was called for cross examination.

"Miss Caney, did you know, or have you ever met Freddie Dean, Michael Watkins or any other defendant prior to the alleged attack at the Dean residence?"

In a much more composed manner she answered, "No, I did not."

"Are you sure?"

"Objection, Your Honor! The question was asked and answered. Mr. Blue is badgering the witness!"

"Objection sustained. Move along Mr. Blue."

Danford Blue gathered his thoughts. "Miss Caney, which defendants are you testifying are responsible for attacking you and giving you all of those bruises?"

This seemed to catch her off guard. "I ... I really don't know. It was dark and I couldn't really tell." She looked towards her father and brother as if to get their approval for her response.

"Well, if it was dark, ma'am, how can you identify all of these men and boys as the ones that did these horrible things to you?"

Panic was beginning to set in. Deborah had to come up with something quick.

"I saw them when they came into the door."

"Well, who raped you first?" Danford began to press. He knew she was lying and he could peep through the crack. He had to kick the door in now!

"It was him!" She pointed at Freddie. She was reaching for a good lie to control the damage that Danford had created. "Then it was him, and him, then him ...!" Deborah was indiscriminately identifying each defendant, growing bolder by the second.

Danford kept prying. "Ma'am, didn't you just testify that it was too dark to see who was beating you? How, then, can you tell who raped you?"

"The light was on at the front door! Only the back light was off! I saw'em. I saw'em all." Now she was defiant.

"I never touched you!" For the first time, Hamburger stood and yelled out, "You lyin'!"

Judge Agar slammed his gavel. "Sit down young man!" The outburst had caught everyone off guard, including the deputies. Up to now, only Freddie Dean had shown any outward emotions during the trial.

Hamburger was forced back into his seat and strapped in. Surprisingly, the spectators barely flinched. The judge grinned with satisfaction that the procedures he had put into place would be sufficient to carry on.

"Counselor, please control your clients. Any other outbursts and he will be removed from this courtroom until the end of this trial. Do you understand?

"Yes Sir."

Any momentum was now lost. "Sir, I have no other questions for this witness."

All that was left was a short list of character witnesses for the defendants, none with any meaningful testimony. Now it was in the hands of the jury.

The mood drew solemn in the cramped holding cell just outside the courtroom.

"Why did ya'll have to fuck her up like that Jeff? She won't gonna say nothin'." Freddie Dean was bitter and resigned to their fate.

"Man, we didn't touch her. That bitch didn't have a scratch on her when we dropped her off. As a matter of fact, I was kissin' her when that got damn dog come out barkin' and took out a piece of my leg. Old man Caney must have seen us when we pulled up and sent the dog out. I damn sure won't gonna hang around and get shot so I peeled out. Her old man must have fucked her up like that. You know how he feels about us."

Total silence.

It didn't last very long. The 2 hours seemed like 2 minutes. The jury was back with a verdict.

As the chain gang was led back inside, Hamburger scanned the entire room hoping to get a glimpse of his parents or maybe Baldy for support. No one was there.

"Have the gentlemen of the jury reached a verdict?"

Kenny Goins stood bold and statuesque. "Yes we have, Your Honor."

"Then, how do you find the defendants?"

"We find the defendants guilty as charged, Your Honor, on all charges!

There was a small clatter of hushed anticipation as the verdict sunk in and Judge Agar wasted no time pronouncing the sentence.

"Will the defendants please rise for sentencing." Everyone rose but Freddie. Two deputies snatched him up and forcefully held him erect.

"After careful consideration of the heinous nature of this crime, I hereby sentence these individuals to death in the electric chair. You all will be immediately transferred to death row at the Powhattan Correctional Facility where this punishment will be carried out 3 months from today. May the Good Lord have mercy on your souls."

Newspaper reporters and spectators scrambled out of the courtroom to report the verdict. Photographers remained behind to capture the melee of the state troopers trying to coral the doomed defendants out of sight. The judge and jury posed for personal photographs.

News of the verdict spread quickly. Baldy was devastated. His good friend Hamburger was going to lose his life because of one stupid mistake.

He wouldn't even get the chance to say goodby.

****

Snapshot

Inner City Blues
The Adventures of Corey Colson

The Bluff, a ten-block area in Northwest Atlanta, has blossomed into one of over 400 drug dens throughout the metropolitan area. Open air markets dominate these neighborhoods, with loosely organized dealers and runners protecting their turf with guns and intimidation. They also served as fertile training ground for up-and-coming teenagers to learn a lucrative trade.

Corey Colson studied the inner workings of the crack trade and quickly moved up the ladder as a trusted runner. He circulated between 10 crack houses delivering "bombs"; large packages of cut up $5.00 and $10.00 capsules for sale. After picking up the proceeds he returned to The Bluff for his payout. $400.00 to $600.00 a night was a lot of money for a 16-year-old high school dropout.

He was on the top of his world. Corey soon bought an old "63 Chevy Impala to shorten his time between houses with no driver's license or tags. He slithered deftly from one destination to another. Each day's receipts totaled in excess of $12,000.

With no air conditioner working, Corey pumped up the volume on his cassette player in route to his first drop. Soon he noticed a car following closely with no lights on. He quickly sobered up when he spotted the familiar shadow of a police car that glistened under the street lamp. Up to now everything was relatively routine. After a few violent killings and robberies, patrols were increased in the area.

Corey stepped on the gas and the Impala roared to life. The police activated it's lights and 2 other cars joined the pursuit. The narrow streets turned into a bumper car rink as the cars carved a path to nowhere in particular. After putting a little distance between him and the police. Corey pulled into a darkened driveway and laid down in the front seat.

Sirens and police chatter dominated several blocks as the dragnet scoured house after house looking for Corey. There was nowhere to go.

Suddenly, a German Shepard in full police regalia leaped into the passenger side window barking and growling ferociously. It happened so fast, Corey was trapped. But instead of attacking, the dog sunk his teeth into the bomb and began shredding and eating it. Corey was frozen with amazement as the Shephard completely ignored him, devoured and slung cocaine throughout the car.

After a few tense seconds, the dog stopped barking and began to moan. Corey gathered anything he could salvage and abandoned the car. He slipped through the maze of fences and backyards and joined the other spectators on the sidewalk. He nervously stuffed the tattered dope package into his pants and stealthily sauntered among the gawkers.

Two policemen ran towards a patrol car holding what at first appeared to be a small child having violent convulsions. As the trio got closer, it was obvious it was the police dog being rushed to the medics for life saving oxygen and critical care.

Herman the police drug enforcement canine officer died the next day from a drug overdose.

Corey "Buster" Colson became a living legend on Proctor Street. He had survived the manic chaos in the Bluff for another day.

****

Edgar Caney and his son quickly packed Deborah's suitcases and slammed the trunk shut. As she walked out the front door, Deborah took a last, long look at the beautiful rose garden she and her mother had worked on so painstakingly during the spring.

Before getting into the back seat, she turned to her father.

"Daddy, I don't see why I have to ..." and 'wham'! Caney slapped his daughter so hard that her hat flew away several yards into the street. Billy Joe, his nephew, never took his hands off of the steering wheel.

"Girl, you done shamed this family for the last time. I should have killed you when them niggers dropped you off. And iff'n you say one word to anyone how you got them bruises on your face, you'll be sorry you ever were born. Now git in that car and tell Sally we'll be down there in a week.

Deborah sank slowly into the back seat and closed the door.

"Now Billy Joe, ya'll have a safe trip to Macon, ya hear!"

"Yes sir." Billy Joe floored the gas petal and fishtailed into the street. Deborah Marie Caney was never seen or heard from again.

At least not alive.

****

The death sentence delivered to the defendants, dubbed "The Henryville Seven" by the local newspaper, was appealed to both the state and federal courts on various grounds, including being denied a change of venue, lack of time to interview witnesses and the ultimate rush to judgement. The appeals were denied on all accounts and the case was returned to the local court for adjudication.

National Media outlets had sickened of the antics that were prevalent in many courtrooms in the south, so they retreated to the relative safe confines of their own local stories. It would be much too dangerous for them to pursue any type of fair justice for the condemned.

They were left to fend for themselves.

Impending death, sanctioned by the state, is both agonizing and debilitating; especially when you are innocent. Being locked up only feet from your ultimate demise can wrench from your mind all conceivable episodes of the circumstances that put you there in the first place. The last meal; an utter farce to human sacrifice. The death march that takes place in front of all of those that follow. Being strapped into the chair; your entire life-works flashing into your mind to find some type of closure for what is to come next. And the final act, when the signal is given to pull the switch on a life; the searing pain from head to toe; the blood in your veins fleeing the sizzling swords that rip your intestines apart so quickly that death does not come soon enough.

And then the deed is done. It repeats itself regularly in places like this. And for the innocent, it can never be undone.

As Hamburger's day arrived, the routine was no different. But to everyone's surprise, on this day, "Old Sparky" would be cheated from the Grim Reaper's playbook. Hamburger's lifeless body hung from a pipe running across the ceiling, his prison shirt clinched snugly around his neck. Written on the wall above his bed was a message:

"I WILL SEE YOU IN HELL"

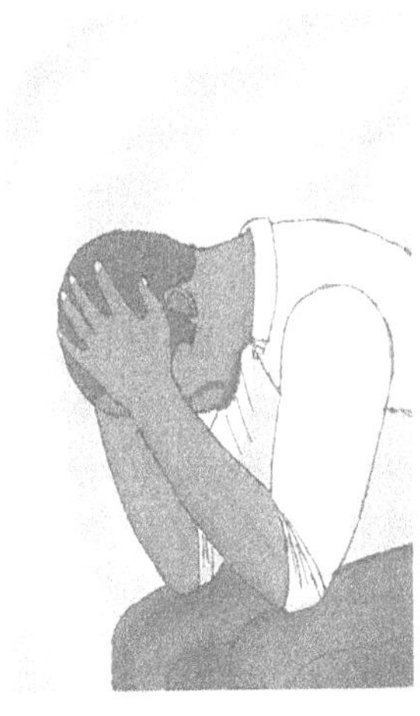

PRESENT DAY

Norfolk, Virginia

Robert Woods reflects dejectedly on the past several years. Even with a college degree, he still found it difficult to navigate the numerous encounters with the police for rather minor offenses. The loss of his childhood friend Hamburger had left him abrasive and unreceptive to compromise in dealing with authority figures. Deep seeded anger would periodically boil to the top, dooming his brief marriage and forcing him to retreat to his small apartment. After brief stops in Columbus, Ohio and Chicago, he settled for a teaching and coaching job in Norfolk, Virginia.

The racial divide in the country has morphed into increasing confrontations between blacks and police officers, with often deadly consequences. The Klan (KKK) had long ago traded in their white hoods and robes for business suit and police uniforms. Even educated minorities were relegated to conciliatory appointments; most others are steered into dead end social programs like subsidized housing and food stamps. Further destabilization of black communities is finally complete with the dumping of crack cocaine in Los Angeles neighborhoods to fight a CIA sponsored war in Nicaragua. Very public congressional hearings were held, but no government or private individual is held accountable.' The scourge of this newfound drug quickly spreads from coast to coast, but ultimately achieves the desired consequences. Crime in black communities ultimately rise tenfold, giving politicians and police a blank check to employ even military style tactics to confront any black person in these communities. After decades of increasing shipments of the drug throughout the country, even today, the drug can readily be found openly on many street corners.

The tremendous amount of money has even spawned several gas stations and liquor stores in these neighborhoods to cash in on the phenomenon by selling the drug paraphernalia to do the drug. Many people caught with the instrument are never questioned where it was bought, obviously giving free reign for the store owners to participate in the scheme. Ninety percent of the stores are run by Asians and Muslims that neither hire black people nor worry about the consequences of their actions. Even they are acutely aware that in this country, you don't have to navigate the legal complexities if they continue to "grease the palms" of their regulatory conspirators.

Robert thought it was strange that in a country as technologically astute as The United States, the deterioration was allowed to go unchecked.

"Hey brother, what's going on?" It was Officer Daniel Phelps of the Norfolk Police Department, a local agitator with a reputation of greeting black people with some unwelcomed engagement for his amusement.

"I'm not your brother!" Robert shot back immediately, and kept walking towards the mall downtown. He was not in the mood.

"Ah, come on Brotha', I'm just trying to be friendly. Ain't nothin' wrong with that, is it?"

"I told you I'm not your brother. But, I might be your daddy! What's your mamma's name?"

Phelps' face immediately turned blood red. His partner barely had time to stop the car, He jumped out and pinned Robert against the pharmacy building and arrested him for disorderly conduct. At his trial, because of 2 similar encounters with local police, he was convicted and sentenced to 10 days in jail and fined $500.00.

Three days after his release, Robert angrily sped off to Richmond, Virginia. This latest arrest had a devastating effect on him. During his incarceration, his most constant thoughts were what will most certainly happen if these types of confrontations continued. He knew he would not back down.

He came up with a plan.

After about 90 minutes of frantic lane changing, Robert turned onto Broad Street in downtown Richmond. He was still steaming and seemed dangerously on edge. As he pulled up to the Chanberlyn Street Law Building, he slowly began to calm himself by taking deep breaths. This was not the time to come unglued.

Robert went into the building and scanned the directory. He took the elevator to the fifth floor and walked up to the receptionist.

"Good afternoon, sir, how may I help you?"

"I would like to speak to Mr. Danford Blue please."

The young lady was slightly startled, but responded, "Well sir, I'm sorry to inform you that Judge Blue lost his fight with cancer over 2 years ago. His son Charles runs the firm now. Would you like to speak to him?"

Robert was disappointed, but not deterred. "Yes, I'll talk to him."

Baldy sat down and looked admiringly around the room. On the walls were pictures of a young Danford Blue, shaking hands with local dignitaries and progressively moving towards his later life and retirement. He had never met Danford or saw a picture of him, but he sure looked regal in his robe. He had retired as a municipal judge for the city of Richmond.

On the wall to the left was a family photograph, including a young, bucktooth Charles and three older girls. Sporting a black bowtie, it was obvious that Charles would be groomed to take the way of his father. Baldy smiled as it reminded him of how at one time, he too, had also admired his father. But his parents were long gone and the frustration with his present situation ultimately refocused him to the task at hand.

The door abruptly opened and Baldy was escorted into the cavernous complex of offices. Legal aides and clients were shuttled about, with a symphony of ringing phones and measured chatter throughout the building. Finally, the massive office of Charles Blue.

"How are you Mr. Woods? How can we help you today?"

"Well, Mr. Blue, when I was growing up, your father represented a few friends of mine in a rape case over 50 years ago. I don't know if you have ever heard of the "Henryville 7" or ..."

Charles eyes widened. "Oh yes! I do remember that case. I was only about 3 years old when daddy went down there for that trial. Man, daddy never got over that mess. The way those men and boys were railroaded, it set daddy back for a long time.

I don't think he took another case for months. I think that case was the main reason why daddy became a judge. With all of the hangings and random killing going on back then, that's the only way he felt he could make a true difference. Did you say you knew some of the men?"

"Mr. Blue I knew ALL of them. But the one named Duane Williams was my best friend. He hung himself after the trial."

Charles sat back in his chair and his forehead pushed up deep wrinkles of interest. He was now curious about what this stranger really wanted.

"Well, what is it you want from me, Mr. Woods?"

Baldy took a deep breath.

"I want to sue The United States of America!"

Baldy waited, but there was no obvious reaction from Charles. He looked Baldy straightforward and asked bluntly, "Why?"

"I think this country owes black people, from slavery, all of the lynchings, beatings and everything else that has gone on in this country for almost 500 years. I have a college degree, I've worked as a teacher, a supposedly respected member of society, but as long as I live in this country, I will always be a nigger."

Charles Blue: "Well, Mr. Woods, I know you are aware that this tactic has been tried before and has been shot down by every court in the nation. Paying reparations to black people just isn't going to fly. It's a lost proposition."

Robert Woods: "Mr. Blue, I am not asking you to sue just for reparations. I am talking about repatriation.

Charles was intrigued. This was a different take on the whole issue. Most black folks were still waiting for their "40 acres and a mule" since shortly after the Civil War.

Charles Blue: "Why here and why now? It seems to me that you have been able to make a pretty good life for yourself. I mean, what are you trying to accomplish?"

Robert Woods: "All my life I have had to fight to survive, being bussed from this school to that school, all of the name calling, the police shootings. And yes, I have been able to carve out a small piece of the pie, but it comes with a price. I remember when my friend Hamburger hung himself in that jail cell waiting to die for a crime that he didn't commit. Yeah, he was in the wrong place at the wrong time, but the last time I checked, the legal system turned a blind eye to what really was going on. Can you imagine the sheer terror he must have felt, waiting to die for something he didn't do. He was just 16 years old and I will never get over that. I don't want to die and my life means nothing. I've seen enough.

Charles Blue: "Then why not just buy a plane ticket and leave? I'm pretty sure if you did a little research, Mr. Woods, you can very easily find a country of origin by simply taking a DNA test, apply for citizenship and be on your merry way. There's Liberia, Nigeria, Sierra Leone. Take your pick.

Robert Woods: "Our ancestors were slaves and not every black person in this country has a chance to escape the poverty and oppression we all have dealt with.

Robert Woods: "... You have to know that most black people don't have the money or the means to make the move. And even if this little venture fails, I'll still do what I have to do. Almost every day, I hear people talking about being fed up with the system. You can't legislate the way people think. It's no mystery that white people are getting pissed off about all of the crime and killings going on and they have made their voice heard with the vote. Things will never change.

Charles Blue: "Mr. Woods, what you are proposing would be time consuming and very expensive. I don't think that it would be in my or the firm's best interest to take on something I'm sure is going to fail. Then what? This comes up every 10 years or so and it gets tripped up coming out of the gate. No, I don't believe I can help you."

Robert stood up to leave.

"Charles, you know that friend that I told you about that hung himself in jail before his trial? The young lady that accused them of rape was already screwing two of the men. Everybody in the neighborhood knew about it. She just got caught. So you see, I'm not going to waste another day waiting for some dickhead cop or loudmouth politician to fight an imaginary war against innocent people that don't want to be here in the first place. I have no hidden agenda. I know that's what you're thinking. The Christians and Muslims can kill each other for all eternity. I don't care. I choose to move on."

"Well, Mr. Woods, I hope you are not upset that I'm not interested. We can still be friends and ..."

Robert broke in, "I guess I overestimated you, Mr. Blue. When your daddy came down to Henryville, we know he worked real hard for those guys. Nobody would take the case and he did a lot with the nothing he had. But, I do know he knew he still had a lot of people depending on him. As a matter of fact, there are a lot of people that got away with shit 40 or 50 years ago that are just now coming to trial. That's because some people don't just give up. Sometimes you have to kick the door in when somebody is trying to lock you out.

"I'm sorry I took up so much of your time today, Mr. Blue. Have a good day!"

Robert shook Charles' hand. As he walked to the door, he was sure Charles would call him back for some kind of late reprieve, but it didn't come. He fired up his car and headed back to Norfolk, Virginia.

Snapshot

Ray Winslow pulled into his driveway after a long 3 weeks on the road. He delivered furniture store displays to various retailers around the country. As he stuck his house key into the front door, it swung open, and his sometimes friend, Jeff Hall greeted him.

"Hey buddy, welcome back! I just finished fixing your pipes under the kitchen sink. Man, you should have seen all of the shit that came out of there."

Ray didn't answer. He knew the pipes Jeff was cleaning weren't in the kitchen, but were located in the master bedroom with his wife.

"Come here for a second Jeff." With a guarded grin, Jeff followed Ray to his car. Ray reached into the glove compartment, grabbed something, and tossed it to Jeff. It was a bullet for a .45 caliber handgun he kept with him on the road. "Jeff, you were able to catch that bullet, but the next time I catch you here, the next one will be traveling a lot faster!" Ray walked back to the house and slammed the door so hard that the night light shattered.

Jeff never returned.

Ray Winslow was on the boat.

****

The Wharf Nightclub in the Inner Harbor was really jumping in downtown Baltimore, Maryland. Young and older couples danced lively to "golden oldies" from all of the top artists. Rap music had proven to be too dangerous for leisurely entertainment at night for most of the country, so this outlet served as a welcomed respite from the daily grind of the workplace.

After his frequent run-ins with the police in Virginia, Robert Woods retreated to the relative quiet of the Maryland suburbs to continue his teaching career. At the Wharf, there were no drooping pants, random gunfire and scripted skirmishes that usually crept into other venues where younger crowds gathered. Things began to slowly return to normal for him and his weekends were mostly spent there until the wee hours of the mornings.

Robert and his newfound love, Lisa Milton, cruised down the Northwest Parkway to Garrison Boulevard. It had been a great night of drinking and dancing and both were looking forward to a good night's sleep. They had met at the new high school for teacher orientation and were an instant couple.

Robert pulled into the driveway at 3917 Bateman Avenue, but noticed a strange car, with the park lights still on, sitting in front of his neighbor's house. He got out and walked around to the passenger side to open Lisa's door. As he got a closer glimpse, he noticed it was a brand new Corvette Stingray with Virginia license plates. Cautiously, they started up the sidewalk to the house.

"You're a hard guy to find!" It was Charles Blue, the lawyer from Richmond. He was obviously drunk and looked disheveled, but made sure Robert could see him clearly under the street lights.

"Charles? Charles Blue? What are you doing here?"

"Been out on the town. That nightclub, The Wharf, it's a pretty nice place. I've been trying to locate you for the last several months to talk to you. You got a minute?"

"Sure, come on inside. Take a load off."

"To tell you the truth, Mr. Woods, I really need to get back to Richmond. But I would like to talk to you for a few minutes if I could."

"No problem. Lisa, go ahead inside. Everything is ok."

Robert waited until Lisa closed the door and stepped towards Charles. "How can I help you Charles?"

"That conversation we had in my office a couple of months ago has been on my mind and I can't quite shake it. I was just wondering if you might still be interested in pursuing it."

"Man, that was 2 years ago. I thought you weren't gonna get involved."

"Things change. From on top of my perch, I really didn't see any justification for moving forward. But as time went on, more and more people were calling the office complaining about Klan marches, the police killings and the slow response for justice. The legal system has even started to squeeze me and some of my employees just for listening. And two weeks ago someone left a severed hand on my front porch. My kid freaked out. I had to ask my wife to take him away until we can sort this out."

"Damn, that's fucked up! What does the police say?"

"Right now, nothing. I get the straight line bullshit about a disgruntled client, but I don't usually represent drug dealers or anyone with shady stories. I don't have to. Lately, a lot of clients have seen a serious increase in police brutality, evictions, a lot of things that have mostly flown under the radar. But with the election of this new president, the pressure has been ramped up and mostly black people are feeling the pinch. It was a clear message. But I'm not backing down."

"Sorry to hear that man, but where do we go from here?"

"I'm heading back to Richmond to shore up the law firm, get a team together and then get back to ya. It took my best investigator 3 months to find you so I'll need your contact information. We'll file the briefs with the appropriate court and get the process going. You, Mr. Woods, will be named the plaintiff, so there are a lot of issues we have to work out in the meantime. When can you get to Richmond for a couple of days?"

"I'll need at least a couple of weeks. Midterm exams are coming up and I don't want to put a substitute teacher through that. Let's do it after the first of the month."

"You know, Robert, this is going to stir up a lot of ill feelings all over the country, maybe the world for that matter. There is a lot of rough road ahead. I hope you are ready for this."

"Don't worry about me. I'm ready,

****

Snapshot

Skid Row, Los Angeles

Carlos Riviera and James Desmond weaved and bobbed through the maze of novelty shops and food stands, frantically peering behind to see if they were being followed. Satisfied they weren't, they continued on towards the Union Mission homeless shelter.

"Man, that was sweet!" Carlos reached into his pants and pulled out the 6 watches he had stolen. "Ha, ha. When I punched that Asian bitch in the face, I thought I killed her, man. She should a never grabbed me."

"Look Carlos we can't keep doin' this shit every day! Sooner or later we gonna get caught!" James came to Los Angeles from Denver, Colorado looking for a new start. The gangs in the Little Five Points Area had made it hard to avoid trouble, so his mother put him on the bus to save his life. All he found was a steady stream of everything he was trying to stay away from, all in one location. Skid Row. A tent city, vibrant with any vise at your whim and call. Their daily activity was getting high on crack cocaine, stealing for extra money and feeding themselves on the backs of the many charities or churches that cater to the homeless.

"Things are a lot better in Santa Monica, Carlos. Why don't we just catch the bus and do something different?"

"No way, man. I was born here on Skid Row and I'm gonna die here on Skid Row. I mean, we got a place to stay, free food and all the dope we can smoke. I ain't goin' nowhere!"

Just as Carlos finished, a Los Angeles police officer flashed his lights and pulled up in front of them to cut them off. Carlos quickly shoved the watches back into his pocket. Officer Jeremy Bates stepped from his patrol car and pointed his baton.

"Stop right there fellas! Keep your hands where I can see them!"

Carlos bolted down the street towards the maze of blue tarps and convenient alleyways. Almost startled, James took off behind him. But, after only a few steps, Officer Bates grabbed James by his shirt collar and slung him to the hood of the police car. James panicked. He elbowed Bates in the mouth, blood and teeth spraying everywhere. He broke free and started to sprint down Los Angeles Street towards the Union Mission. Bates recovered and fired 2 shots in his direction.

"Shit! I'm hit!" The pain was excruciating and his right arm grew numb. Blood began to trickle in a steady stream. He stopped and turned towards the officer and 2 more bullets tore through his upper torso. Before he could utter another word, a third bullet exploded out of the side of his head.

"Why did you shoot him? He ain't got no gun!" People on Skid Row are fiercely loyal and quickly pounced on the opportunity to seize the moment. Word of the shooting spread and small marauding bands of crackheads and drug dealers, thieves and anyone else familiar with the daily skirmishes on Skid Row sprang into action. They began to ransack and pummel the mostly Asian and Hispanic merchants in the immediate area, snatching merchandise, jewelry and anything else they could get their hands on.

Police units arrived to assist the injured officer and restore order. James body laid in the middle of the street until the coroner arrived.

James Desmond is the 37th unarmed black male to be killed by police In the United States in the last 14 months. It would soon get worse.

Richmond, Virginia

(2 Weeks Later)

Robert steered his car off of Interstate 95 onto Laburnum Avenue. A few blocks east to Ridgeway Drive, he arrived at Chandler Manor Estates. After entering the code, the massive gates opened and he continued on to Charles' sprawling mansion at the end of the street.

"Nice house, Charles," he thought.

Several cars were already there. License plates from New York, Pennsylvania and Ohio were front and center. He walked up to the front door and rang the bell.

"Thanks for coming!" Charles Blue opened the door immediately. "The team is anxious to meet you. Come on back."

Robert followed Charles through the spacious living room to a back office. He looked in amazement at the large pictures of Danford Blue, reminding him of Charles several months earlier. Charles opened up the double doors to a phalanx of workers scurrying about; some eyeing laptop computers and others retrieving manuscripts and textbooks from the law library. Everyone came to an abrupt halt as the men entered.

"Ok everyone, I want you to meet the man responsible for this very important exercise. This is Mr. Robert Woods, a high school teacher and coach in the Baltimore City School System. I'll just need to introduce you quickly and you can return to your assignments. Afterwards, Mr. Woods and I will confer out back for most of the rest of the day, if that's alright with you, Mr. Woods."

"Sure, Mr. Blue. I'm anxious to get started."

"Great! Lets start with Mrs. Ling Na Cho. She is in charge of Media Relations ... Logistics. She'll be responsible for scheduling all, or most of, our strategy sessions with the press. Starting today, if anyone has any information that we need to communicate to the outside world, it goes through her. No exceptions!" Ling slowly bowed and said nothing.

"Next we have Mr. Wayne Parks, Commercial Transactions, He will be researching the cumulative history the impact of slavery has provided this country for the last 400 years." Parks was a slight, shy man from the prestigious Blagovich and Westchester Firm in New York City.

"A pleasure to meet you, Mr. Woods. I hope to be a tremendous asset to you."

"Let me see. Ok, Mr. Joel Chance, Constitutional Law; Clayton Hodgeson, specializing in mediations and negotiations; our Civil Rights attorney, Lawrence Andrews and Dr. Joseph Mitchell. He is the head of the Resolution Institute in the College of Administration Law at the University of Akron. He'll be the team leader and designated troubleshooter. Everyone has already started their research and we will meet bi-weekly until all of the paperwork has been filed with the proper court. Mr. Woods, do you have any questions?"

"No, not right now. It looks like you've got the ball rolling. What do I need to do?"

"Well, you and I will have a brief meeting out by the pool to discuss some things that are sure to come up in the very near future. Dr. Mitchell can handle this."

Everyone sprang back into action. A little bit of anxiety came over Robert as the sheer magnitude of what was about to come began to sink in. He would have to refocus himself to see it through.

Robert followed Charles to the patio and immediately took in the peaceful surroundings. An Olympic size swimming pool looked inviting, but there was much more important work to be done.

"Can I get you something to drink, Mr. Woods?"

"Sure. But call me Robert back here. Do you have any White Label Scotch?"

"You bet. There's a notepad on the table. Take a look at it and you will see a list of security concerns that are bound to pop up. The Aryans in Idaho, Republicans and Democrats for their own agenda will probably offer some manner of resistance. Even the NAACP will come after us because they feel that black folks have never had It so good. We've got to be ready because this will open up a lot of deep wounds on every side. Are you totally sure that this is what you want to do?"

"The way I see it, there is no turning back now. Over 150 years after the Civil War we are still trying to do things that was supposed to integrate us into this society. Shit, not only are we being killed on a daily basis, a lot of people are still fighting for their right to vote. A lot of white people will never accept the fact that an ex-slave could possibly tell them what to do. Ask the Klan. Do you read the bible?"

"Yes I do. Why?"

"Do you remember what happened to Moses when they found out he was a Jew? The Romans stripped him of everything he owned and sent him back to the brick-making kiln. At the rate things are regressing in this country, how long do you think it will be before the forces that be decide it would be too dangerous to cede any more rights or privileges. I would rather take my chances in an African country than spend the rest of my life looking over my shoulder for the next police car or racist idiot that wants to turn back the hands of time."

But Charles did not relent. He had expended a lot of resources to convince his colleagues to buy in to this endeavor. There would be no turning back.

"Ok, Robert. I can see that. But lets look at the probable drawbacks. First of all, there are about 20 million black people in this country. Thats a lot of people to move. Realistically, even if a tenth of those would go, what happens to the rest that stay here? What happens to the social programs? The civil rights groups? Professional athletes? Musicians? Entertainers? I know rappers talk a lot of shit but I don't think the prospect of taking a dunk outside is going to be very appealing to them. Are you willing to tackle all of this and come out on the other side with your head up?"

Robert was reticent of what could lie ahead.

"If people don't want to go, so be it. At least they have a choice. Up to now, everything has been decided for us. Public housing; Affirmative Action; the list goes on. We were turned loose like free range chickens going in a million different directions. It was on the backs of our great grandparents and the many slaves before them that this country was built. Even the Indians eventually got federal lands and even casinos. The Japanese that were held in concentration camps during World War II got some kind of compensation. And who wants to be the first person to grace a Slave Museum! That should fill our kids with a lot of pride. We will be the laughing stock of the world when that happens."

"I just needed to gauge your true commitment. Once the paperwork starts, a lot of people are going to come after us and it could get quite dangerous. I need to know you're going to be there.

"I'll be here to the end, Charles. You have my word."

"Then, there is one more thing we need to discuss. Security. I'm putting together a team for around the clock protection. Once the word gets out about this lawsuit, forces will come out of the woodwork to see that it fails, or, pass for that matter. It's going to take a couple of weeks to fine tune the details, so be ready. I'll do everything I can to keep your schedule as routine as possible, but there can't be any deviations from the script. This issue is going to fray a lot of nerves, so be patient."

"I'm ready! Lets do this!

****

Chris Dalton gunned the beat up Nissan 280zx at the stoplight, barely missing a homeless lady pushing her shopping cart across the street. He was unfazed.

"Fuck! Late again for work!"

The tires screamed and moaned as he turned into the parking lot of the Baltimore Star Newspaper. He breezed by the security guard at the front desk and into the elevator.

"Dammit, this might be my last day!" he thought on the slow ride to the 8th floor. The doors opened up to a bustling mix of reporters and whirling conversations about their daily business; getting out the news. Before he could get to his desk, Chris spotted his boss, Editor Jason Blair, and a few other staffers walking towards him. He started banging on the drink machine to pretend he was already there.

"Goddam machine takes my money every day!" Chris made sure he said it loud enough for everyone to hear. It didn't work.

"Where the fuck you been Chris?" Jason Blair didn't even look at Chris' direction. He had already been by Chris' desk. "I'll be back in 2 hours. Be in my office!"

Chris Dalton is a features writer for the Star, but spends most of his time smoking marijuana and bar hopping in the inner Harbor of Baltimore most nights. His claim to fame was to expose police kickback payments provided by drug dealers loyal to the East Side Crip Gang in Poe Park. The report garnered him a national investigative reporting award and decent job security for at least a couple of years. Time was just about to run out.

"Way to go Clark Kent! Whatcha gonna do now?" Jerry Speaks is the resident blow hard that anchors the late night news for the Star's affiliated television station. The "last place" rated news cast for the metropolitan area. He was always looking for a scapegoat to unleash one of his childish tantrums on.

"Maybe now we can get some real work done around here!"

The thought of beating Jerry to death briefly flashed into Chris' mind, but he had bigger problems. He had to do something quick to keep his job.

Chris bypassed his cubicle and dejectedly stepped into the breakroom. It had a bank of television monitors that were turned down and news highlights crawling across the bottom of the screen. He could barely focus. The Jamaican Rum from the night before was still playing serious tricks on his mind. But one thing was for sure: when his boss returns, he had better be sharp as a tack!

Suddenly, "BREAKING NEWS" flashed onto the screen. The United States Supreme Court has granted a review of the landmark litigation Woods versus United States of America. Chief Justice Warren Bradley released the following statement: "The Supreme Court feels that it is important for all citizens of this great nation, to finally rest the debate, whether reparations or resettlement of African-Americans should, or could be an enforceable obligation under the constitutional law as presently mandated. This decision will be final and binding"

It was like a cold slap in the face for Chris. He rifled through the refrigerator, of which nothing belong to him, opened a diet soda and bit into someone else's cold cuts. He reached into his pockets for a note pad and pen to write down the details: The court will convene in Richmond, Virginia in a special session, allowed for decisions deemed "Landmark Cases". Opening arguments will begin in six weeks. The entire proceedings would be televised internationally in order to promote transparency.

Chris wrote a note for his boss and left it with Jason Blair's secretary; "Gone to Richmond, Va. The Woods Case got some feet. I'll keep you up to date. Chris D."

Chris was outta there. The trip would give him time to cover ass. He still had enough connections to weasel his way into the courthouse media pool. It would garner him a front row seat to the proceedings and, hopefully, save his job. It was his only shot.

Charles Blue, the lead attorney, had successfully argued for a compromise agreement, which kept the trial from reaching the United Nations mediations court. It was a calculated risk, but Charles thought that any decision will be binding and would survive any legal challenge.

'Woods vs the United States of America' became a worldwide phenomenon. Everyone had an opinion. Surprisingly, even racist groups like Arion Guard and the KKK came out immediately in favor of the referendum. "I'll give them Niggers everything I got if it would shut them fuckers up! They lazy as fuck anyway!" That was a sentiment announced by Gary Gray, the grand Pointiff of the white nights in Belgrade, Louisiana.

The black community was split as well. Most wanted to stay, but a very vocal and surprisingly large number supported the idea of returning to Africa to make a contribution. Professional athletes, musicians and the entertainment industry lobbied heavily to quash the hearings. Tell Tarzan and Cheetah "Hello!" for me was their dismissive and derisive response to the proposed legislation.

The split made for strange bedfellows. Blacks who wanted to stay felt uneasy about the coordinated attacks spewing from the hate groups, right wing politicians and others who tried to align themselves with the cause. Clandestine organizations rented billboards and television and radio advertisements to sew the virtues of "self-determination".

One of these groups was the White Knights of the Holy Order run by Edgar Caney Jr. of Henryville, Virginia. Yeah, that Edgar Caney Jr., who had inherited the leadership of the group when his father passed a few years earlier.

Presently, he was discussing a very important issue with a Martin County Sheriff's Office deputy.

"Now Edgar, you and your daddy was the last ones to see your sister alive. Now you know and I know what happened to her, but there are a lot of people asking questions that could put a crimp into what we are doing about the investigation.

Edgar was drunk and smelled of moonshine. Just the thought of his sister, Deborah, brought back a flood of onerous memories and filled his bloodshot eyes with rage.

Suddenly, a familiar face flashed on the television screen. It was a picture of Robert Woods and the lawsuit that was beginning to galvanize the nation.

"Got dammit, man it's that nig ..." He caught himself before the deputy heard him.

"Now look here Terry Lee, me and my daddy didn't have anything to do with what happened to Deborah and it plum broke my momma and daddy's heart when she didn't show up in Macon. We was in Henryville hunting and never made it down there because she never wrote us back. She just disappeared." All the time, he never took his eyes off of Robert's face, silently fuming to his rotten corpse how the two events were playing out at the same time. Deborah's skeletal remains were discovered in Butts County at the excavation site for a local apartment complex. The coroner found 6 bullet wounds in her remains. A gaping hole was found in her skull.

Butts County, had become the unofficial dumping ground for freed slaves after the Civil war. As the federal government began to squeeze the locals about the the discovery of Deborah Caney's body, it ratcheted up the pressure to begin to solve the identity of hundreds of victims.

Still, Edgar was totally mesmerized by Robert Woods face. When he told a local deputy that he thought Robert had rocked his car several years ago and got away with it, he never got over it. Then his sister shamed the family by screwing black boys and men.

"Well, I know that boy was probably there when they fucked my sister, the bitch!" Edgar said under his breath. "I need to find him and stick this blade in his ass."

Deputy Terry Lee was oblivious to what Edgar was saying and kept talking.

... "Let me tell you something Edgar, we got your cousin Billy Joe down at the police station on an assault charge and he is singing like a rooster on Saturday night. He said he done a favor for you and your daddy a long time ago. You might want to git your story right. If he starts shooting off at the mouth, a lot of people could get hurt, if you know what I mean. You gotta do something."

"Does he got bail?"

"The judge ain't set it yet. His lawyer is ole Avery Mason on Stuart Street. Billy Joe done told the prosecutor that he has some information about how Deborah Caney ended up in them woods down there. These niggers from the college is doin' free DNA work for the state. If you got any shit laying around that you need to get rid of, you better make it happen."

"Thanks Terry. I'll take care of it. Just don't let him talk to nobody else for a couple of days, and I mean NOBODY!"

"Ok. But this conversation never happened." Terry Lee grabbed a soda off of the table and left.

Edgar Caney had to come up with a plan. He knew his cousin Billy couldn't stand another felony conviction. A guilty verdict would mean life in prison and Billy was weak and careless. Instead of dumping Deborah's body where he was told, he panicked and dug a shallow grave just off the highway.

Edgar didn't know who he was madder at; Robert Woods or his stupid cousin. He did know which one he had to deal with first.

Billy Joe Caney.

Not since the Civil War has any action so galvanized the nation; and the world for that matter. Brother debating brother. Interracial squabbling about the pros and cons for maintaining the status quo: "Black people have never had it so good." To ... "It's time we as human beings take the opportunity to put all of this away forever. We can never move forward if we keep dredging all of this stuff back up."

After a few weeks on the Sunday morning news circuit, it was decided, for his safety, there would be no more public appearances for Robert Woods. Death threats were coming in by the thousands from anonymous sources. Some even suggested Robert swim back if he wanted to go that bad.

"Robert, I've got some bad news." Charles Blue had called and came quickly to Robert's house in Baltimore. "I think we have a leak somewhere and until we can find it, I'm going to probably move you until the trial. Sorry man. I mean, it's too dangerous to ignore the fact that somebody is feeding info to the Attorney General's Office. That can never be good."

Robert wasn't completely shocked. He had seen quirky signs that things were not all in their place.

"Where do we go from here?" Robert asked.

"I don't know, but I am going to dissolve your security team. I think that's our compromise."

"No problem. I don't trust Stacy Rogers anyway."

Charles was caught a little off guard. "Why would you say that?"

"I came home early the other day from a workout and noticed footprints going to and coming from my bedroom door. I also take a few pictures before I leave to check for anything that's been moved. If you get down on your knees, you can see footprints. It's a little trick I learned from a college buddy of mine. You get the carpet cleaned and shampooed and you can see all of the new impressions for about a week. Nobody is supposed to be here."

"Damn bro! I didn't want to tell you, but that's who we've been watching. I'll take care of it. Give me a couple of days."

"Charles, how about you let my buddy put together a small crew that he can trust. I mean, it's my life we are talking about here. And it takes you off the hook."

"I don't know man. A lot is riding on this and it has morphed into something that is probably bigger than both of us now, A small breach could not only mean your life, but a lot of others. I don't think that it would ..."

"Before you say anything else, hear me out. He has already proven his worth. His Name is John Ashley. He's the head of security at Baltimore Prison downtown. He's the one that showed me the carpet trick back in college when our refrigerator was getting robbed. It worked every time. At least let me talk to him."

Charles Blue thought for a moment. He looked out of the bay window and into the spacious front yard. Stacy Rogers, head of security, was talking to someone on the phone in his car. He walked over to Robert and whispered into his ear. "Alright, tell your friend the first thing I want him to do is a bug sweep of the place. But don't call or talk to him here. Meet him anywhere you want. We need to find out who, or what, we are dealing with."

Robert followed Charles' eyes out to Rogers' car. He nodded yes and started to peer wearily at his surroundings.

He understood.

****

Snapshot

Mughali Abasi Mosque
Chicago, Illinois

Matawa Babur sat in his office at the Abasi Mosque contemplating his next move. Homeland Security was tightening the screws on all of the mosques and various hate groups around the country because of the upcoming trial. Background checks and stepped up surveillance severely hampered his movements. Matawa's real name is Jasper Kidd, a federal prison parolee from the Mississippi Department of Corrections in Jackson, Mississippi. He converted to Islam to stay alive. But he got back to his drug connections as soon as he was released. He used the mosque to store heroin, cocaine and a tremendous amount of cash throughout. His drug mules were constantly harassed at the front gate. Two were arrested.

He knew it was only a matter of time before he got a knock on his door.

Just then, a group of men came by his door talking loudly.

"I think The Prophet has clearly dictated that we, as black Americans, should stay here and fight for a share of this country and not retreat to Africa. Our future is HERE!"

"But think about the great changes we can bring to Africa, Brother Abdul. Women are getting kidnapped and raped, deadly diseases ... I mean, what are we to do in America, sell beanpies and newspapers for the rest of our lives? What is the honor in that? You afraid to be a man?"

The two men stepped towards each other and were quickly pulled apart.

"You're wrong!" Ramat yelled back. "Brother Babur is right. We must be ready to strike at the infidels at a moment's notice. You must be vigilant and true to faith. That is what makes me a man."

"Please, my brothers. The Prophet will hear you." Mohammad whispered. This is not the time and place for division. If we are to stay united, we must not confront each other with disrespect. Let the court decide and I am sure things will play out in our favor."

Matawa had heard enough. It was now or never to make a break for a new start before his small drug empire came crashing down. He gathered a few belongings and over 1 million dollars in cash and headed out under the cover of darkness.

****

John Ashley found 4 recording devices and 2 cameras in the house. Robert was shocked. Beads of sweat raced down the side of his face as John went over his options.

"What do you think Ash? Is this guy Rogers working for the other side?"

"It would be my guess that he is your man. He is the only one that has constant access to your house." John was a no-nonsense kind of guy that didn't believe in a lot of fluff when it came to dissecting the obvious. "This stuff is not easy to get. The bugs are standard CIA issued 360's but the cameras are, no question, a high end product from the FBI Surveillance Unit. No metal parts. Standard issue. You can't just get them at Radio Shack. It looks like you've made the big time buddy. I say you need to get out of here as soon as possible."

"Where do I go? What about court? And what about Charles Blue? If it is Rogers, what happens to him?"

"Calm down. Not the end of the world. At least not yet. Give me 48 hours to move. Don't talk to anyone about this. Not even Blue. Leave everything as it is so we don't tip them off that they have been compromised. I'm gonna put 2 men on you until it's time to get out. Go to work, shop and stay with your regular routine. After everything has been set up, I can get you out to a safe house. And one more thing, I don't take checks. Too easy to trace."

"The foundation that's funding the litigation is paying most of the bills. That's Charles Blue's department. He ..."

John interrupted, "Then I'll handle it. I don't want you talking to anyone about this."

"Thanks John. A lot is riding on this. But can I ask you something?"

"Sure Rob, go ahead."

"You got any kind of opinion about this lawsuit?"

John took a couple of seconds to think about his answer. "You know, people have an opinion about a lot of things. My opinion about this lawsuit is just that; my opinion. What I think doesn't matter. What does matter is that you totally trust me and my team to do the right thing by you. I don't think it would be a good idea to get emotional about something when it could affect how I do my job. Your life, my life and the lives of my team have to be focused on the task at hand and that has to be the basis of this commitment. We can talk about this when the verdict comes in over a drink. How about that?

"Good enough for me. I trust your judgement."

"Great. I'll stop by tomorrow. Remember, don't even use your phone until you see me."

"Ok."

****

"Now Edgar, you need to be careful with that knife. You know I don't like knives." Billy Joe Caney thought he was going to meet his lawyer for a strategy session before he gave his deposition about the murder investigation of Deborah Caney. Instead, he was greeted by the gruesome sight of his lawyer, Avery Mason, staring wide-eyed with his throat cleanly sliced from ear to ear.

He knew he would be next.

"Billy Joe, Billy Joe ... what do you want from me?"

"You been talkin' to the police down there?"

"I won't gonna' say nothin' about you and your daddy. I just wanted to get outta jail. I had to come up with somethin' because I'm lookin' at life on this assault charge." Billy Joe was hoping against hope that he would be spared.

With his back turned to Billy Joe, Edgar swung around with his right hand with a machete. The sword cut off his cousin's head so fast, he was still standing when his head hit the floor. Edgar left out the front door.

Next stop: Richmond, Virginia and Robert Woods.

Richmond, Va.

The trial, Woods vs. The United States of America, started with opening arguments for the government. Winthrop Hagens extolled the many accomplishments of blacks in America and their contributions.

"... Slavery was, and always will be, an onerous chapter in our history. This nation will forever be grateful for the countless sacrifices black people have made for the advancement of our ancestors. But, each man, woman and child is afforded the opportunity to achieve their life goals unimpeded in their quest for happiness. Our forefathers that fought and gave their lives for the freedom of every person that calls themselves an American today instilled in us the virtues of righteousness and fair play. This litigation is not only an unnecessary plague on the progress of this nation, it stains the progress made by a most powerful people that has provided lawyers, doctors, engineers and even a president to count among their achievements.

"Today, we ask you to continue the many good works that have been done. Help us to heal the wounds opened by this very unnecessary legislation. Men and women of this court, today we ask you to put to rest the division that has infiltrated the very soul of this most grateful nation and put to rest any attempt to brand America as anything other than what it represents; ... the land of the free and the home of the brave.

Charles Blue was not impressed. His statements were brief, but intense.

"... From where you view the world lies the problem, Mr. Hagens. The doors that have been open to most black people have led to prisons and poverty. For over 400 years, and even today, there still exists an attitude of dependence and uncertainty. Uncertainty about our place in this society which has not been determined by us, but for us. Public housing. Food stamps. Police harassment. These are the factors facing many black people in this country today. No matter what you see when you look out your window, we only see blight and despair. This is not the first chance this country has had to make things right. The '40 Acres and a Mule' legislation was shot down as quickly as it was implemented, leaving black people with little options but to flee in no particular direction. And with the recent developments around the country, it is painfully obvious that black people and whites will never live side by side as equals in this country.

"We are asking you to give this proud people an opportunity to finally guide their own lives; to make their own way, and die in their native land. That is all we ask."

"Remember, the world is watching."

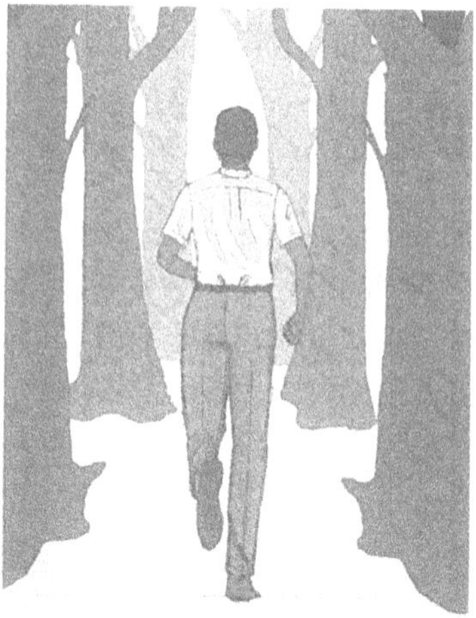

The proceedings were broadcast. Blacks in London, Paris and Toronto, Canada were keenly following the drama unfolding daily. Their governments were in the crosshairs of similar lawsuits that were pending and wanted to get a glimpse of what could be heading their way.

Hagens called historians who talked about the founding of the country from the landing of the first colonists to the various programs designed to integrate all minorities into mainstream society. More than once he mentioned the enormous expenses to enable immigrants to make their transition into the 'melting pot' that the United States had become.

Charles Blue concentrated on the high number of incarcerations and the quality of life issues that crippled black communities. "... No matter what social status most blacks achieved, they will forever be identified as a nigger in this country."

There were heated exchanges on both sides and Charles was often cited for contempt of court because of his biting and inflammatory cross examinations. Every day the trial offered new fodder for conversations at the dinner table, water cooler and bars everywhere. The Supreme Court Justices had the unenviable task of playing referee and at the same time render a decision that would ultimately serve as a measuring stick as to the perception of being a country exploiting the vulnerabilities of a rudderless people or the worldwide champions of goodness and mercy for all.

The trial also offered a smorgasbord of information that a lot of people didn't know; the return of many freed slaves to Africa shortly after the Civil War, the explosion of insurance companies that sponsored the ships and slave auctions, the prominent role of African war lords that offered up their own people for little or, in most cases, nothing except the sparing of their own lives. They also exhibited the crack pipes and other drug paraphernalia sold by a bevy of store owners of Middle Eastern decent that turned black communities into open air drug markets and the most dangerous communities in the country. Almost all of the service stations involved only hired blacks to clean up the parking lot or dump the trash. Virtually none were hired to work behind the counter.

Snapshop

Inner City Blues
The Adventures of Corey Colson

After numerous narrow escapes from the police in Atlanta's notorious Bluff neighborhood, Corey is sidelined from his usual dope runs. Three years on the street and various relatives' couches has reduced him to penny-ante hustles just to eat.

"Buster" Colson spends most of his days hustling and the night looking for shelter among the many condemned houses and abandoned buildings that dotted the streets. Buster had hardened and even his own family didn't trust him.

"I'll be back!" he kept telling himself.

Corey turned down Ashby Street for one last pass through before heading in for the night. A small crowd gathered at the Corner Market as usual.

"Hey! Buster Colson! What up man?"

It was Greg Upshaw. His nickname is "One-up" because he always tried to one-up or tell a more fantastic tale when swapping rip-off stories at the local hangout. He also got caught most of the time so everyone at the store broke out in different directions.

"Hey, Buster! Holdup"

Greg caught up and tapped buster on the shoulder.

"Look, One-up, I ain't got time for nothin' right now. I'm tired, broke, hungry and with no money. I'll see you later."

"Hold up man. Look. This is sweet! I done already hit this place twice and the lady is out of town. All I need is a little boost and it will be over in five minutes."

"No good, bro. I'm on probation and if I get busted, that's 2 years. Count me out."

Just then a loud growl came from Buster's stomach to remind him of the past few days of no money or food. One-up laughed out loud.

"Daaaamn, Man!! It sounds like your little intestines is trying to eat your big intestines. When was the last time you ate?"

"Don't start. Something will break for me. I'll check you later"

"Wait, wait! One-up grabbed Buster's left arm to stop him and he immediately regretted it. Buster's large frame pinned him against the store's stonewall and his left elbow pressed tight against One-up's neck.

"I said, no way! Now leave me alone!"

"Okay, okay! I'm sorry man. I just thought you might want to get in on this easy lick. I mean, you wouldn't even have to go in. Just look out for me. We'll split it half and half. But I can find somebody else. No problem."

Buster thought hard about it as he slowly let One-up off the wall.

"Man, are you sure this is straight up?

You gonna go in and out and all I have to do is be look-out. No shit?"

"Yeah, man! No shit! Buster! You know I wouldn't bullshit you man! Straight up!

"Alright. Let's go. But if this is some of your usual tall tales, it's not going to end good for ya. You got that,"

"Sure Buster! Let's go!

It was a short 2 blocks and a left on Simpson Ave. One-up led Buster down a dark alley to the back of a small green bungalow. One-up carefully surveyed the windows and smiled back at Buster.

"As soon as I get in, go to the end of the driveway and watch out."

"Well, you just hurry up and do what you got to do."

One-up nodded and turned to the window. It was slightly cracked open. All he had to do was jump up and grab the window sill and pull himself up. Old lady Griggs always left her window open on sweltering nights to catch a cool breeze.

One-up took one step back and leapt for the windowsill, but his hands slipped off and he slammed into the side of the house. Knee-first. He crumpled to the ground in pain.

"Oh shit, that hurt:"

"What the hell are you doing man? You gonna wake up the whole block!"

One-up limped to his feet.

"Shh, keep your voice down. I know, just give me a little boost up and I can get in. The window is open. We here now. WE might as well go ahead".

"Come on One-up. Lets get this shit over with."

Buster bent over and One-up straddled Buster's broad shoulders and was lifted towards the slightly open window. After getting one last burst of strength, One-up raised up the window and grabbed inside the sill with both hands and prepared to hoist himself inside.

Suddenly, there was a deep, muffled thud, One-Up removed his hands and Buster found himself stumbling back and forth then sideways with One-Up staring in disbelief at his smashed fingers that hung loosely from his hands. The shock of the gruesome sight sent him to a loud, hysterical scream as he kicked and swayed, still perched on Busters shoulder.

"Aaaaay, Oww, Buster, let me down!"

One-Up looked in amazement as 3 of his fingers on his left hand hung limp and bleeding profusely. Seeing this, he forced Buster to the ground and started banging on every door in the area to get help. As dogs began to bark loud, lights began to spring to life in the neighborhood.

Buster picked himself up off the ground and watched in amazement as One-up disappeared into the summer night, not waiting for anyone to come to the door because of the severe pain. He resembled a crazed cartoon character crisscrossing the street banging on doors. The pain was excruciating. Buster briskly walked away in the opposite direction and disappeared into the night.

"What happened?" Buster thought to himself.

Ms. Griggs has set the bait because of the previous break-in by leaving her window open and sitting in the darkness with a brand-new hammer from Home Depot. The next day she found a lot of blood splashed on her window sill. And One-up's middle finger laying on the floor lifeless. No one ever came by, including the police to inquire.

One-up lost 2 more fingers that had to be amputated at the hospital.

His new nickname is now Two-up, because they were the only fingers left on his right hand.

Corey "Buster" Colson's legend is intact.

****

Robert Woods had a front row seat to the festivities. Yet, the proceedings had isolated him to the point that he was alternately praised and hated. People on both sides of the aisle were satisfied with the 'status quo'. The only communication he had with the outside world was through his security team.

John Ashley took over all of Robert's movements for the immediate future. Stacy Rogers was reassigned to the courthouse so he could be watched. John asked Fred Cook, a highly decorated Army Ranger, to watch Rogers. Fred worked as a credentialed custodian so that he could gain daily access to the courtroom. Doug Good and Donnie Musk were added for protection and transport operatives for the duration of the trial. They turned Robert over to Rogers on court days inside the plaintiff's chamber. They watched Rogers meticulously for any sign of compromise. When court was over for the day, even Charles Blue was kept in the dark about Robert's whereabouts.

Robert never spent two nights in the same place. John had secured a number of safe houses between Baltimore and Richmond. Even homeless shelters were in play. Local theater makeup artists were hired for subtle changes to hopefully avoid recognition.

John Ashley thought of every possible scenario that could arise.

Conservative talkshow hosts exploited the movement by professing the virtues of segregation and empowerment. Even some white liberal politicians crossed the aisle and openly aligned themselves with the cause. Tempers and confrontations exploded across the country. National Guard and reserve units were deployed to the outskirts of virtually every major city. An uneasy calm was restored only temporarily, as forces looking to capitalize on the moment moved to stoke fear and intimidation. Arguments by both the government and the plaintiff were substantially reduced in order to expedite the trial.

Hundreds of thousands of people began to converge on Richmond as the trial began to wind down. Those that couldn't make the historic trip congregated in their state capital or huddled around the television to witness the trial.

Remey's Sports Bar and Grill was teeming with lawyers, reporters and hangers-on to get their daily feel for the trial. Chris Dalton, of the Baltimore Star newspaper had retreated nightly to the bar as the unofficial court spokesman and interpreter. He had temporarily staved off his firing by thrusting the Star back into the national headlines. He spent most of his time gloating about his previous conquests. One observer began to take note.

Edgar Caney was not impressed.

He was watching the daily drama from his perch at the main bar. The shots of vodka weren't having the desired effect, so Edgar frequently retreated to the bathroom for the flask of bootleg in his shirt pocket. As the concoction began to work it's magic, his mind began to wonder to the simmering thoughts of his sister Deborah and the shame he had to live with. Suddenly, he composed himself against his emotions and got back on task. The Martin County Sheriff's Office was looking for him since the unexplained murder of his cousin Billy Joe and his lawyer.

"Daddy, give me the strength to do what I gotta do." Edgar stepped back into the bar.

Edgar started watching the frantic scene of reporters and lawyers debating the merits of the trial. Chris Dalton served as the unofficial moderator and instigator; playing both sides of the debate to up the ante for the ratings.

A tall black man in a very expensive Italian suit slipped Chris a note. After quickly scanning the piece of paper, he grabbed his coat and bolted for the exit. Intrigued, Edgar walked out behind him and watched.

"Are you sure she is here?" Chris was excited, reaching into his pocket for his keys. "What's the address?"

As Chris jumped into his car, Edgar was hot on his trail. He knew if Chris Dalton had a tip, everyone at the bar would be the last to find out. He got into his beat up Dodge truck and followed.

Edgar made sure he stayed a good distance behind, but never out of sight of Chris' sports car. Chris slowed down at a large apartment complex in the northwest section of Richmond. He walked up to Apartment #6448 and knocked.

"Yes, Miss Williams, it's Chris Dalton from the Baltimore Star Newspaper. Would it be possible for me to step in and ask you a few questions about your brother Duane? It will only take a few minutes and I promise you nobody knows you are here."

Seconds later, he was inside. The name sounded familiar, but Edgar couldn't quite piece it together. He stepped out of the truck and creeped up to the living room window to get a better look. He couldn't believe it. Sylvia Williams, Duane "Hamburger" Williams' sister was in town for the trial. She had largely stayed out of the limelight, but was on the official trial access list and was granted a provisional pass to the proceedings.

Edgar began to hyperventilate as the sight of his sister Deborah began to again invade his mind. His obsession would peak, then reside, and common sense would intervene. But only briefly.

"This could be a nice little bonus for us daddy." Edgar whispered to himself. He could feel himself slowly rise and his hormones flared. He was going to get some of his revenge tonight.

Edgar walked back to his truck and waited. Thirty minutes later, Chris walked briskly to his car and sped off.

As soon as Chris was out of sight, Edgar knocked on the door.

"What happened, Mr. Dalton? Did you forget ..." That's all Sylvia could get out. Edgar pushed his way inside and flashed a menacing grin.

"Now Edgar, you ain't got no business bein' here. My brother Hamburger is gone and ain't coming back. Why don't you just leave me alone."

"Well, Miss Sylvia, that shit your fat ass brother and his friends did plum sent my mama and daddy to an early grave. Not to mention what it did to me!" Rage began to return to Edgar's eyes. Then, like a an eagle swooping down on it's prey, he was on top of Sylvia, ripping off her clothes.

"Now bitch, you gonna feel like my sister did when all of them niggers was fuckin' her. Except mine is gonna be a whole lot better. Then, we even. That alright with you, bitch? Edgar backhanded her, almost knocking Sylvia conscious. She fought desperately to stay awake." And what that city cracker doin' here? You and him got a little something goin' on?" He started massaging her tits and wildly kissed at her neck. When Edgar sat up and started to unzip his pants, Sylvia reached up and violently slapped Edgar, drawing his anger to the rim.

"What was he doin' here, bitch?" Edgar punched her in the nose with his fist and it instantly broke. Darkness crept into her eyes. There was nothing left to fight with.

Suddenly, a knock on the door.

"Miss Williams. It's me, Chris Dalton from The Richmond Star. I forgot to leave you my card." He turned the knob and walked right in before he got an answer. Sylvia couldn't speak. She was fading fast.

Edgar barely had time to roll off Sylvia and behind the couch before Chris spotted her limp body on the floor.

"Sylvia! What happened! Are you OK?" Chris reached into his pocket for his phone and cautiously scanned the room for an intruder. Edgar crawled up behind him and raked his knife across his throat and blood sprayed everywhere. Even Edgar was beginning to get a a serious rush as the killings were starting to add up.

Blood in her eyes kept Sylvia from actually seeing the attack, but now she knew it wasn't going to matter. She would be next.

Edgar took the knife and put it into Sylvia's hand. After peeking out of the front window, he stepped into the darkness.

"One down and one to go."

Snapshot

Prestone, Alabama

It was the classic staredown; a grizzled lioness sizing up a small gazelle through the high grass of the African plains; the hardened gunfighter staring down the latest attempt by a young kid about to die trying to make a reputation; and Marilyn Fortson about to exact her revenge for a crime she never saw coming.

The quick and mysterious death of Marilyn's parents had sent a painful shockwave through her entire body. She was a daddy's girl, but her three brothers had schemed for decades to alienate and discredit anything she accomplished. After the final funeral, her father's, it was discovered that Marilyn Inez Fortson had been completely removed from the wills of both parents. Her three younger brothers threatened their parents with abandonment if they didn't agree to the terms.

Marilyn is a very successful trader at the New York Stock Exchange and Alex, Jeremy and youngest brother Oscar resented her success. They terrified their own parents on virtually every front in order to gain control of their estate. The Fortsons were powerless to resist.

What made Marilyn even more angry was that none of her friends or relatives stepped in to help. The signs were there. The Fortsons were seldom seen in church or at any of their regular activities. Nobody in Prestone wanted to get involved.

Oscar died shortly after his parents from an aggressive form of acute kidney failure. The doctors couldn't determine the cause of his illness, so they classified his death as "natural causes". Alex and Jeremy began fighting over their dead brother's estate, even kicking the front door off it's hinges over a dispute over the furniture.

It was a public embarrassment.

Marilyn soon figured out that all of the fuss was over only one thing: wills.

Her brothers were devising a diabolical scheme to enrich themselves by appointing themselves as power of attorney or the executor of the estate to ransack and steal from anyone they thought were vulnerable. Now it was plainly obvious that even their own parents were victims.

Nine months after Oscar's death, Marilyn slipped back into Prestone, Alabama and introduced her oldest brother Jeremy to a brand new wooden Louisville Slugger baseball bat she had bought just for him. He didn't see it coming. While he was unloading his groceries, Marilyn hit him in the back of his head with the force of an avenging angel, killing him instantly.

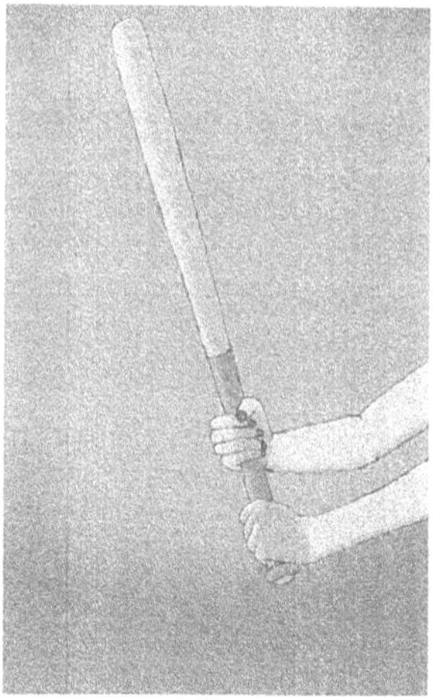

Jeremy wasn't found until a work detail from the local jail discovered his battered Jeep Cherokee in the deep marshes of Lake Elaine about 30 miles away. His brother Alex had grown very suspicious of his whereabouts and contacted local police. Over the vigorous protests from Alex, the coroner ruled his death as an accident. At Jeremy's funeral, Marilyn glared menacingly at Alex through dark shades so he couldn't see the immense hatred she had for him.

It didn't matter. He knew he was next.

It was late, but Alex couldn't quite make out the dark figure in the woods across from his house. Somebody was watching him through a patch of trees next to the church. Panicked, he ran from room to room, window to window, locking and double checking as he moved.

Marilyn picked up a large stone and hurled it on the roof. The loud thud halted Alex in his tracks, freely wetting himself in the process. He followed the sound of the now rolling stone into his gutters. "My phone! Where is my phone?" While he was locking up, Alex also turned out the lights and forgot where he left it. Then he remembered.

"Damn! In the fucking car!"

Marilyn moved closer and onto the back deck, watching the frantic antics of her brother. She would have laughed, if not for the seriousness of her task. Alex found his .44 Magnum pistol and crouched behind his couch, sweating profusely, his heart racing.

Marilyn threw a large boulder through the back sliding glass door. The crash startled Alex so bad that he bolted for the front door. In the darkness, he tripped over the coffee table. As his right hand hit the floor, he squeezed the trigger and shot himself in the throat.

Marilyn slowly stepped into the kitchen with her 9mm drawn, scanning the room for her brother. There he was, clutching his throat with both hands, staring up at Marilyn staring down at him. His eyes widened as he realized what had truly happened to his brothers. He made one more attempt at taking a breath, but it was too late. He was gone.

Making sure she didn't touch anything, Marilyn slowly backed out of the house and calmly walked to her car. It was over.

Marilyn Inez Fortson was on the boat.

****

Mutawa Babur has transformed back to Jasper Kidd, his birth name, and left the Chicago mosque with over two and a half million dollars stuffed in a green duffle bag. Paid informants had begun to erode the trust in the Muslim community and he felt it was time to break camp before his major drug network would be exposed.

Jasper zig-zagged down the backroads of Illinois and Ohio, finally pulling into the Dew-Drop-Inn in Border City, Kentucky. He had barely slept for the past 22 hours. Each passing car or flashing light was a constant reminder he was a fugitive on the run. His plan was; he didn't have a plan. The way the Woods trial stoked the fires around the country, Jasper would truly have to sleep on it.

****

John Ashley traded in the crisp white dress shirt for a more casual uniform that would be more suitable for the task of protecting Robert Woods during the entire trial, but also maintaining his responsibilities at Baltimore Pen.

"Ash, the warden wants to see you in his office."

John didn't even look up. He was looking over some of the surveillance photos his team had taken of the crowds that assembled daily for the trial. He wanted to make sure no one was overlooked.

"O.k. I'm on my way."

John took the back stairs down to the third floor and knocked on Warden Hal Jenkins door.

"Johnny! What's goin' on? Sit down for a sec. I need to talk to you."

Jenkins turned serious, closing the door quietly. "Some of your staff has noticed a little sting in your step recently. Is everything alright?"

"Well, I'd be lying to you if I said this protective assignment with my old college friend is working out. I mean, it's just a lot of footwork that has to be done and I'm not really at liberty to talk about it. You've got my word. I'll make things right with the goons."

"Are you sure, Johnny? Some character came by the intake desk the other day and asked for you. When we asked for an I.D., he brushed us off. Said he was working for some security consulting firm. He didn't stick around long enough for us to check him out."

"Did he give you a name?"

"Angela just got Terry Stroud. He didn't show anything."

"What about video?"

"We got him downstairs. And we got him heading north to Princess Anne Street using the video grid. He was driving what looks like a standard issue government Crown Prince SUV. Couldn't get a tag number. We saved it for you. Go see Angela."

John took the elevator to the operations center on the first floor. Operations Manager Angela Marshall knew John would be there. John was well liked and respected by his co-workers, and they appreciated him being there for them.

"Morning Captain Ashley! I have already pulled up the video you want to see. I'm heading for a quick briefing. Make yourself at home."

"Is there anything I need to pay closer attention to on this thing?"

"I don't think the guy is who he says he is. Beyond that, it would be probably best if you saw it yourself. Could be somebody you know."

John turned on the monitor and glared at the screen. Almost immediately he recognized Stacy Rogers. He had made no attempt to disguise himself. He also noticed Rogers was careful not to touch anything with his hands. Either the FBI was flouting its power or Stacy Rogers had his own agenda to complete. Rogers had to know that security measures were state of the art around, and inside, the prison.

"Rogers must be getting desperate.", John thought to himself. But why?

****

The Baltimore Star Newspaper

Baltimore, Maryland

"What do you mean, 'Chris hasn't shown up'? Find him! Call his mother! Got dammit, that boy is fuckin' pissin' me off! The biggest story in a hundred years and that punk goes missing." Editor Jason Blair has just been told that Chris Dalton hasn't reported to his usual perch for the daily trial briefing.

"... Get Harold down there as soon as possible! Call the local police and hospitals! Don't just stand here! Somebody find Chris!"

Staff members sprang into action. It wasn't long before the grim news was retrieved from the national wire service: "... City of Richmond Police are reporting that a Richmond, Virginia reporter for The Baltimore Star Newspaper and a local woman were found murdered in an apartment the female shared with her boyfriend ..." A picture of Chris Dalton's driver's license on the screen sealed the deal.

Meanwhile, Chief Homicide Investigator Lane Castor continued to review the grisly scene in Sylvia Williams apartment.

"Two double murders inside of a week," Castor pondered. "I think these murders could be related to the 'All Points Bulletin' we received on that Edgar Caney guy. I knew this shit would end up on our doorstep with this trial going on. I need the Henryville Police on the phone now, and get me somebody from The Star that knows what that reporter was doing here."

Word of the murder quickly made the national headlines and stoked more riots around the country. Attorney General Winthrop Hagens requested a recess for the day to decipher the latest tragedy that could possibly entice even more violence. Charles Blue brought Robert Woods and the rest of the legal team up to speed.

"We're going into Emergency Recess. A pool reporter and a lady from your hometown was killed last night and the police want to make sure it doesn't have anything to do with this case. Robert, do you know a woman by the name of Sylvia Williams?"

Robert thought for a second. Then ...

"Yeah! I know her! I grew up with her and her brother. He was the one I told you about that hung himself in jail for that bogus rape charge. What happened?"

"Don't know yet. Hagens and I will get together later and wait for a full police report. I agree with him. I think we need to find out if there's a loose cannon out there we need to deal with. I'll contact John Ashley when we get something."

Robert Woods was spirited away by a member of his security team to a garbage truck at the back of the building. To his surprise, John Ashley was in the driver's seat.

"John! What's up?

"Robert, we got a problem. We can't talk here. We're going for a short ride. I don't think it would be a good idea to hang around here." John didn't wait for an answer. He rammed the truck into gear and down the back streets of South Richmond.

"Who is Sylvia Williams?", John asked.

"I just got through talking to Charles Blue about her. He didn't go into any detail about what happened to her. What's going on?"

"She was found murdered this morning with a Baltimore Star newspaper reporter. Is she anything to you?"

"Well, she is the older sister of my best friend that hung himself in his jail cell in order to escape a trumped up rape charge. Why would anybody think it may have something to do with this case?"

"The reporter was a guy by the name of Chris Dalton. Does that ring a bell?"

"Nope ... nothing."

"When was the last time you talked to Sylvia?"

"Man, not since her brother's trial. The whole family moved away to get away from the Klan. Nobody heard from any of them in years."

John thought for a second. "There are a lot of people on both sides that are going to come after you with their own agenda. I am going to reduce the size of your security team and temporarily keep you in the courthouse with 24 hour supervision. Somebody might be trying to flush you out. Until I can get some better info, this is the best route. You good with that?"

"What about Charles? What will he say?"

"It's not up to Charles, Robert. It's up to you. It's your life we're talking about here. Not his. I am the only one besides yourself that is immediately concerned about your welfare. We have to be on the same team."

Robert didn't hesitate. "John, whatever you say, goes! Lets finish this."

John and Robert picked up dinner and returned to the courthouse.

Sporadic violence flared up, not only in the U.S., but Canada, Great Britain and Germany also had to go on high alert. The delay of the trial only fueled speculation of a cover-up by the governments to sidestep their moral obligations, as espoused by hundreds of both foreign and domestic terrorist organizations and factions. Even drug cartels weighed in on the proposals. They could lose a lucrative market if the court rulings advanced legislation cracking down on illegal aliens that moved their drugs. Media markets fanned the flames by chasing the 'next great story'. A lot of innocent people lost their lives.

A 72 hour moratorium was granted to allow the U.S. Government and the lawyers for Robert Woods to broker a truce that would be conducive to a reasonable resolution. This decision would not only set the tone for the temperament of future race relations in America, the whole world would take notice.

****

Just outside of the shuttered doors of the Federal Courthouse Building in Richmond, Virginia, Jason Blair, the Editor of The Baltimore Star Newspaper was having a hastily arranged news conference:

"... Chris Dalton was a fine investigative reporter; a highly respected and decorated journalist who pursued a story with unrelenting purpose. He will be truly missed by his newspaper family and colleagues."

"Mr. Blair, what was Chris Dalton's relationship with the Williams woman and does it have anything to do with the Woods trial?"

"The murder investigation is an ongoing process and me and my staff have been instructed not to discuss any details until further notice."

"Henryville, Virginia Police have identified a suspect, but have not released his name. Do you know who it is?"

"Again folks, we can't discuss any information related to this particular case because it involves one of our employees. As the investigation proceeds, we will provide any and all details about Mr. Dalton's movements and motives as they become available. But you can get an up to date briefing on this and other world news at your local Baltimore Star Newspaper stand."

Jason Blair and his entourage quickly left the podium. Now the media was part of the news and the Star's reporters fanned out to find some answers.

****

It was only the second day in the bowels of the Federal Courthouse Building and the pressure of such an immense endeavor was about to drive Robert insane. He stopped watching the nightly television reports debating the pros and cons of the pending litigation.

Since the trial began, Robert had been virtually isolated from the outside world. Forays to morning news shows and brief visits with family and friends had denigrated into constant trial updates, strategy sessions and mostly solitary confinement for his own safety. But John Ashley had put together an elite team of Army Rangers led by Fred "Chiefy" Cook, a decorated weapons specialist with massive biceps, and a host of deadly gadgets. Chiefy was the first, and last, person Robert will see until the end of the trial.

As the government lawyers and Charles Blue huddled to break the stalemate, the country, and the world for that matter, held their breaths. Regardless of a decision, there are forces that are destined to not be satisfied with the final verdict. But this is a decision that has to be made so that it could finally be put to rest. Everyone was guarded about how they conversated about race in order to not be seen as bigoted, insensitive or out of touch.

Meanwhile, John Ashley used a confidential informant to track down background information on Stacey Rogers. Showing up and giving false information at the Baltimore Pen was a serious probe into John's personal or professional life. Both were off limits, in his mind, and would warrant a response. Rogers had access to unlimited resources.

John took advantage of the break in the trial to do a little snooping of his own. Just as the informant had said, Rogers rocketed out of the gate of the Capital Bar and Grill on 14th street in northwest Washington, D.C. in a jet black vintage Shelby Mustang. It was a predictable ritual whenever he got drunk. After narrowly missing a parked vehicle, he sped off towards his Laurel, Maryland home. John frantically tried to keep up with the intoxicated Rogers and nearly lost him several times. The rush hour traffic kept him close.

Rogers eventually slowed and pulled into a half moon driveway in front of a large split level house. He got out and took a long, deep swallow from a flask and threw it back into the car.

John killed the lights on his Maryland state issued Chevy Caprice, intently watching the lights come to life on the first floor. He waited a few minutes and walked up to the door.

"Hello John. Come on in. I've been expecting you." Rogers opened the door before John had a chance to knock. He stepped cautiously into the living room.

"What do you mean, 'You were expecting me.' I thought I did a pretty good job following you." John was already familiar with the driving tactic to identify anyone following. It allowed easy identification of suspected miscreants.

"Well, we got a lot of people working for us too, so we only let people know what we want them to know. You didn't find me, I found you. Anytime an inquiry is made to the DMV or any state agency about active agents, the information is automatically funneled to the necessary bureau chief and is dispatched immediately. I knew what you were up to before you did."

"So, it WAS you that planted the bugs in Robert Woods house!"

"No, I can't take credit for that. And save your breath. I can't tell you who did. But I will give you a little bit of advice. I think you are way over your head on this and this can't end good. If you think the President of the United States is going to bail your people every time things get a little tight, you really don't get it. Its time to stand on your own 2 feet."

John didn't want to get into a debate about the merits of the trial. He found out what he wanted to know. His only concern was the safety of Robert Woods.

"So, where do we go from here, Stacey? Do you know something that I need to know?"

"Know something? I don't know nothing. I work for the government of the United States of America. Everything I do is in the best interest of the United States.

****

Robert Woods' legal team, led by Charles Blue, Professor Joseph Mitchell and Patricia Bryant, put together an enviable display of statistics related to the impact a positive decision would have, not only for the economic progress of most black people, they also cited obscure amendments in the U.N. Charter which call for the return of any displaced people to their original homeland as a result of ethnic cleansing, war or slavery. Even though the amendment was drafted as a mechanism to protect Jews and others affected by World War II, Charles effectively argued that American slaves should also be afforded the same consideration. Since the United States is a fervent defender of human rights, he proposed the country set an example by leading the world back from the brink of racial bigotry.

The government countered with the astronomical costs and the tradeoffs necessary to pull off such an endeavor. Winthrop Hagens, the Attorney General, would require the abolishment of all civil rights commissions, government subsidized housing based on race and most other programs that were draining the budgets of inner cities. They also contacted the governments of Liberia, Sierra Leone and Guinea to gauge their commitment to a possible reverse migration of what was beginning to look like several million people.

After 3 days of rancorous and terse exchanges, the panel reached a compromise. A national crisis will be avoided.

Charles Blue was blown away with the outcome. He bolted from the workroom to deliver the news to Robert personally.

"Robert! It's over! We won! This long journey is final over!"

Robert didn't know what to feel. He didn't really expect to get here. Now that he has arrived. ... now what?

After a long celebratory hug, Charles reached into his briefcase and pulled out a bottle of scotch and a bottle of water. He quickly opened both and handed Robert the scotch.

"I'm drinking water today. I've got to meet the press and work through some other details. But we'll make a victory toast. Here's to a new beginning!"

They each took a long, savory gulp.

"You know, Robert, you'll be a very famous person now. We'll be setting up a live press conference for tomorrow and things will begin to heat up after that. We both could use a good night's sleep and can get together to out the details in the morning. Where's John?"

"He told me this morning he was going to be a little busy. That's all he said. You know John. He's always in work mode."

"Shit, he deserves a bonus! Tell him to call me when he gets in. It's still his show."

Within minutes of the decision, news channels and wire services reported a break in the stalemate. From all over the country, millions of people descended on all highways, airports and train stations to Richmond, Virginia. Efforts to slow down the pilgrimage were futile. People simply abandoned their cars or other modes of transportation and continued their trek on foot.

****

Jasper Kidd emerged from the western mountains of Virginia and smack dab in the middle of a slow moving caravan heading to Richmond. Police and roads were taxed to the point that nerves were frayed towards violence. Numerous accidents backed up traffic for miles in all directions. Any small space that was big enough to get through was in play.

****

Edgar Caney was on the move too. An 'All Points Bulletin' had been issued for his arrest in the slayings of his cousin and his lawyer in Henryville. Local police wanted to question him about the Sylvia Williams and Chris Dalton murders as well. He shaved his head and donned an eye patch in a poor attempt at a disguise. The racist tattoos on his face and right arm would quickly betray him.

****

Master Staff Sgt. Phillip Conover was filled with dread as the eastern sunlight slowly peeped above a cloudless skyline. As the duty clerk in the evidence/property room at the Richmond Police Department, he dealt with the most mediocre assignments a seasoned police officer could expect. His latest assignment didn't come from his watch commander, Zone 2's Captain Adam Stewart. They were delivered to him personally by Silas Bannister, president of Sons of the New Confederacy, or SNC, a secret sect of devoted public and private officials and normal citizens whose main objective is to sew discord and mayhem as needed. The organization has been in existence since shortly after the end of the Civil War and has morphed into the go-to network for organizations like The Klan and segregation proponents throughout the southern and western states.

Conover slithered out of view of the many cameras and stuffed a rifle, fully disassembled, into his workout tote until after work. He had drawn the black bullet out of the hat and had the group's most important take down in 40 years; shoot Robert Woods at the Monument Avenue news conference.

****

John Ashley was furious. With only 3 hours left to prepare for the news conference, he felt it was too risky. Millions of people were expected to invade the city and there wasn't enough time, or people, to protect Robert Woods from the many problems that will certainly come up.

"Charles, you can't be serious! This will be a suicide mission! Even with all of the police and Secret Service and everything else, it still ain't enough. It's just too risky!"

Charles Blue wasn't about to give in. He had rightly invested a lot of time and resources to the trial and reveled in the vindication achieved for the shortcomings of his father in the Henryville rape trial several years ago.

"John, this is history here! We can't just pack up and leave. Now is the time to thank everyone that is responsible for us being here and Robert owes it to those same people to show them that we will not abandon them like all of the rest that have tried to do this and failed. If he is not there, what will that say?"

Throughout the trial, John Ashley and Charles Blue had maneuvered flawlessly past the numerous roadblocks in front of them. Now they were far apart on how to navigate the potholes that are sure to surface.

"Plenty can go wrong here, Charles. Just look around you, man. There isn't enough time to get everything in place."

"And why won't those goons of yours let me talk to Robert? Maybe he'd like to speak for himself. Where is he?"

"Waiting to hear from me. When I turn him over to you, that's it! I can't take indefinite responsibility for him. The trial is over."

"John, you can't quit on me now! We've come too far together. Look, just get Robert to the stage tonight. He won't have to say anything. Let the people see him. At the end of the news conference, you can turn him over to my security team and we can handle it from there. Please John. Help me out here."

John's head began to throb at the prospect of going against his instincts. Many challenges have crossed his path as a security specialist and it wasn't wise to succumb to what he often referred to as 'peripheral bullshit'.

"Alright Charles. We'll be there. Don't make me regret this."

"Ah, man. It'll be great! Thanks John!" Charles opened the door to the conference room and a gaggle of reporters were already waiting. Charles quickly went into lawyer mode, sucking up the limelight that shadows victory. John watched with contempt and left.

****

John Ashley looked around at his 3 man security team, double checking each to make sure they understood what to do.

"We've only got 2 hours to make this thing work, so everybody ready to go?" John turned and didn't wait for an answer. He knocked on Robert Wood's door and walked in.

"Ok Robert, it's showtime."

Robert smiled and headed for the door. Fred Cook slithered up behind him and pressed the chloroform laced cloth around his face and within seconds, he was out. The team scooped him up and laid him on the bed.

Dierk Johan, the head makeup and costume artist for the Baltimore Ballet Company, was ushered into the bedroom with his wares. He was joined by Donnie Musk, a local comedic actor and the subject for Johan's latest project; make Donnie Musk a passing representation for Robert Woods.

This isn't the first time John Ashley has used Dierk's masterful talent to completely fool the public. High profile prisoners and other dignitaries have been shuttled throughout the city and state by diverting would be instigators and media to far flung regions while the true clients were discretely transported in obscure ways. John became the point man in the eyes of both state and federal authorities when it came to maintaining a low profile in high profile cases.

After about 45 minutes the transformation was complete.

"Damn man, when I die, I want you to do me!" Donnie was totally amazed at the resemblance as he looked admiringly at himself in the mirror.

"Get Robert's clothes off and put them on, Donnie. The rest of you get in position for the news conference. Chiefy, make sure everything is ready for the transfer. You and Robert will be on your own."

"I'm on it, John. Good luck!"

John, Donnie, the Robert Woods stand-in, and Joel Macklin headed towards Monument Avenue for the much anticipated news conference. The plan was to get downtown as close to the stage as possible and walk the rest of the way. Dierk had provided clothes from his wardrobe department to help the trio blend in.

City police and several National Guard units were on full display as municipal workers feverishly built the VIP stands in Monument Park. News satellite trucks, mobile police units and firetrucks were used to funnel most of the people converging on the park into a 6 block area surrounding the festivities. Even though Zone 4 Richmond Police were responsible for logistics and access, Zone 2 reserve personnel were activated for backup protection and crowd control.

Phillip Conover's assignment was street level enforcement which allowed him plenty of time to slither down to the old Kimbrough Tobacco Warehouse Building on Shenandoah Street, a mere 3 blocks and within direct sight of the reception stage. Conover opened the back door with a crowbar that was placed in a nearby dumpster by Russ Savage, an enthusiastic member of Civil War re-enactors for several Confederate sympathizers.

Conover climbed to the top floor and walked to the window facing the stage workers. On the sill sat the Chinese made Phuong II rifle he smuggled out of the property room. He pulled up a chair and started admiring the slinder, light weight killing machine that boasted a 3000 to 3500 yard guidance system with uncanny accuracy. His sight lines were unimpeded and the laser scope would light up as the intended target came into focus.

"Piece of bourbon cake!", he said to himself. "Mother fucker won't know what hit him."

****

Deborah Caney laughed uncontrollably as one man after another had their way with her. It got louder and louder until ... Edgar Caney woke up violently, arms flailing, stabbing into the air. It was that dream again. The one that shamed the family name and sent his mother to an early grave. Ever since the trial in Henryville, the curse of his sister's whoreness would creep into his sleep, plodding him to strike out at imaginary ghosts from the past.

After realizing that he must have fallen asleep, Edgar got his bearings and began to slowly edge his truck towards the festivities in downtown Richmond. With only a couple of hours left, he didn't want to miss what may be the last opportunity to get to Robert Woods. As the thought of gutting Robert raced back into his mind, he started driving reckless, forcing pedestrians and slower vehicles out of the way. He didn't see the Virginia State Trooper in the median as he gorged a hole in the masses in front of him.

Trooper Tanger's tag reader began to spring to life and Edgar Caney's mugshot popped on the monitor. He activated his siren and sped onto the busy street in pursuit. Edgar floored the gas pedal and the truck immediately responded. The vehicles careened through the traffic, forcing evasive action by both cars and people.

As they approached the congestion downtown, Edgar got even more desperate, barely missing people and light poles. Edgar barreled right through stoplights, with Trooper Tanger hot on his tail. Cars in front of the chase saw the drama unfolding in their rearview mirror and attempted to get out of the way. Tanger was not so lucky. He scrapped the side of a Nissan Pathfinder SUV, sending the SUV and it's passengers onto the sidewalk and into a large group of pedestrians. Tanger's car careened into the intersection and struck Jasper Kidd's car head on. Both drivers were killed instantly, with Jasper's car flipping up against the Russell Street Drugstore. A very familiar looking confetti began to rain down on the street. It was the hundreds of thousands of dollars Jasper had pilfered from the mosque in Chicago. While a few people tendered the injured, the majority swooped in on the money, further hampering rescue efforts.

Edgar Caney slowed a few blocks later and calmly parked the truck. He scanned his surroundings and continued downtown, melting into the sea of people heading to Monument Avenue.

****

Fred "Chiefy" Cook slipped into his uniform for the Richmond Metropolitan Ambulance Service. He pulled Robert into a wheelchair and rolled him out of the door. The security guards in the reception area barely watched as the pair headed out the back door. Robert, still unconscious, was placed into the back of an ambulance and Chiefy headed for the rendezvous point near the reception downtown.

"They just left!", came over Stacy Rogers radio.

"I've got them."

Stacy followed the ambulance for a few blocks and then turned on the GPS locator attached to the undercarriage. Rogers had paid a lot of money to track the team's movements since the beginning of the trial. His latest instructions weren't from the FBI. As a life member of the Sons of the New Confederacy, he was in a prime position to monitor the movements of Robert Woods' entire security team.

Feeling confident, Rogers backed off of the ambulance so that it slowly drifted out of sight. Background checks were run on all of the men that had direct contact with Robert Woods in case there was a confrontation. The information revealed that Chiefy would be a formidable foe, with weapons and survival training accomplishments that garnered Army-wide recognition, including his face on the regional recruiting manual. He could easily spot a vehicle or person tailing him, even in these congested conditions.

****

"Where the fuck are you, man?" Charles was beginning to get agitated and impatient. "The cameras will be rolling in 15 minutes! You said you would be here."

"Keep your thong on Charles. We had to take a detour to get here. It would be nice if we all got there safe too, don't you think?" John spoke careful, not wanting to banter with Charles now. "We'll be there in about 10 minutes. Everything is fine."

"Ok. I'm ... I'm sorry man. I know I've been a little rough on you lately. It won't happen again."

"No problem, Charles. See you soon." John hung up before he could ask to speak to Robert. The plan was to get Robert to the stage on time, but not allow him to speak. It was Charles show anyway and John had a queasy, unsettling feeling about such an impromptu gathering of this magnitude. If anything went wrong, a lot of people could get hurt or die.

Edgar Caney pushed his way towards the main stage, scanning the area for a glimpse of Robert Woods. Closer and closer he inched, keeping a keen eye out for any police in the crowd. He knew they were there somewhere. Every few steps, Edgar patted the top of his right waistband to make sure his gun was at the ready.

****

The GPS transmitter in Stacy Rogers car began to wildly ping, signaling the ambulance has stopped. As he turned left on Gilpin Rd, he saw Fred Cook retrieving Robert Woods from the back.

Fred wrapped a blanket around Robert and started towards the main stage.

Rogers pulled his car onto the sidewalk and followed on foot. He picked up the pace until he was right behind Fred.

"Running a little late aren't you Chiefy? Now don't turn around! Just stop here." Rogers made sure Fred heard him chamber a round into his Baretta. "You don't mind me calling you Chiefy, do ya?" Robert was still unconscious and oblivious to what was happening.

Rogers snatched the radio off of Fred's belt and slammed it to the street, not taking his eyes off him. "Now, real slow, I want you to push that nigger to the restaurant over there and remember, I know you are a bad mother fucker but if you so much as flinch, you both get it in the back of the head. Move punk!"

Fred did as he was told and started Robert towards the Blue Buffalo Restaurant.

"Playing both sides these days Rogers? I told John you were a worm. What's the problem, you getting behind on your mortgage? I thought you got paid pretty good for all the bullshit you spread."

"Well, you know how it is Freddie Boy. Why not do my job and make a little on the side. Besides, doing a good deed by ending this shit tonight will be all the better, don't you think?"

Fred was seething as they neared the restaurant. Even though people were everywhere, he knew Rogers wouldn't hesitate to shoot. And being a credentialed agent for the FBI didn't hurt either. He had already replayed these scenarios in his mind many times over the years. If you fail these kinds of tests, you don't get a second chance.

"Stop here." Rogers made sure he stayed a safe distance away. Stacy Rogers was a big man, be he knew that if Fred got close enough, it would be over in a hurry. Most people saw Fred's muscles before they saw his face.

"Ooh ... man damn. What happened?" Robert was just easing out of his deep sleep. He groggily looked around for his bearings. Everything is still blurred, and his head was throbbing. The noise and lights began to come into focus. Stacy Rogers stepped into view.

"Welcome back. Seems you took a nice little nap. But please don't make any sudden moves Mr. Woods." Stacy made sure Robert saw the gun barrel pointed in his direction. "Stay in the chair and don't move. You might get to live a little longer."

"Are you serious Rogers? All of these people out here and you're gonna try something stupid?" Robert looked around and saw Chiefy standing behind the wheelchair. Chiefy hadn't taken his eyes off of Rogers since he reintroduced himself. It would only take a split second to make his move.

"Fred, you keep your hands on the wheelchair and don't move'em." Rogers reached into Chiefy's waistband and pulled the .45 long barrel from his hip. "Now, I'll take that can opener you keep in your pants leg. And remember, I know how you think and right now it's best you don't do any thinking at all. I'm good at what I do too."

Robert still couldn't quite figure out exactly what was going on. He could barely see the stage beginning to fill about 50 yards away and the unbelievable mass of people all around.

"What is this about, Rogers? You still mad about losing your job?"

Rogers' anger shot to the top so fast, he slapped the gun barrel into the side of Robert's head. Robert went out again, this time with a deep slash over his left eye. Fred flinched, but just as suddenly, his.45 was inches from his face.

"Too early to be a hero now Freddie. You don't mind me calling you Freddie do you? That sounds a lot more, ah ... gay, don't you think?"

Fred held fast. Robert was hurt, but just out. This isn't the time.

A loud roar came up as Charles Blue and his legal team stepped on stage. Charles looked around nervously for John Ashley and Robert Woods. He finally spotted them about to approach the steps. Donnie Musk was reveling in the limelight as the fake Robert Woods, flashing a wide smile behind the large sunglasses. A spotlight shown on the trio and the crowd went wild. Donnie raised 2 thumbs up, sure to stay in character.

"Don't forget Donnie, keep the glasses on and no talking. You stay in between me and Joel. Understand?"

"I gotcha, John! No problem!"

The men started up the steps, stopping just short of the bank of microphones centerstage. John maneuvered himself in front of Charles' view to keep him from getting a better look. It would be utter panic and pandemonium if he got close enough to see a switch and wasn't consulted first.

Sporting a wide grin, Charles stepped towards the men to greet them. John quickly grabbed him in a tight bear hug and whispered, "Robert has a little bug he picked up from one of the stash houses. We don't want anyone to get too close until we can find out what it is. Go ahead Charles. This is your night too. Do your thing and we can get together as soon as this is over."

Charles was caught a little off guard, but relented.

"Hey! ... no problem." Charles held up his hands and Donnie returned the gesture. He played his part well.

The crowd roared. The noise seemed to vibrate the buildings all along the immediate area surrounding the news conference. Pundits estimated the revelers and detractors in the city totaled in the millions, with hundreds of thousands more heading their way.

****

Phillip Conover's hands began to shake as the activity on the stage began to start. He double checked the range finder on the rifle and took a couple of drags from the cigarette on the window sill. After a deliberate deep breath, Conover flipped on the target focus, bringing John Ashley and his crew front and center. He was sure they would be wearing bullet proof vests, so a head shot is the only option.

Conover steadied the rifle and took careful aim, at first, John Ashley. Then the man he thought was Robert Woods came into view. All that was left to do was to activate the laser sight and wait for the signal to shoot; it will come from a signal flare fired from inside the crowd. The ensuing panic would offer cover for the shot.

****

Edgar Caney has squeezed to within 30 feet of the stage. It was ringed with police and military personnel, but Edgar laughed at the ease it will be to get off a shot at Robert Woods. He slowly reached into his waistband and pulled out the .45, concealing it with his left hand.

"All I need is one shot. Got to make it good."

****

Fred Cook watched small beads of sweat pop up on Stacy Rogers forehead, telling him something was about to happen. With Robert's severe head wound, Fred knew he had to move quickly or they both will soon be dead. With his right hand, Fred reached over and pinched Robert's neck until he screamed out in pain. It startled Rogers long enough for Fred to extend his left arm straight out, activating the spring loaded .25 automatic tucked under his armpit. The gun rocketed down his sleeve, nestling firmly into his left hand. Fred caught the trigger with flawless precision, delivering it's payload in a bright cloud of dust. Rogers never had a chance. A gaping hole appeared where Roger's right eye used to be and he fell straight back, still clutching his gun. He was gone.

The shot set off a frantic melee', including gunshots and a bright red flare from the middle of the crowd. A surge of desperate bystanders stampeded in all directions, many falling dead in the random spray of gunfire. Fred retrieved his gun and knife and checked the wound on Robert's head. He was still out, blood vessels wildly pulsating from the blow to his face and head.

The gunshot had startled Phillip Conover as well. He fired at the scramble unfolding on the stage, taking down 2 people in the vicinity of John Ashley and his men. John and his team ducked low and slithered under the stands to plot their escape. Donnie Musk was hit in his right shoulder and was bleeding profusely.

"Stay calm, Donnie. We'll get you out of here." John scanned the crowd for a place to evacuate Donnie until the shooting died down. "You think you can make it?"

"It hurts like shit. I don't know how long I can take it. My arm feels like it's on fire."

Edgar Caney had missed his window of opportunity too. He fired indiscriminately at the stage in frustration, killing 3 people, including Charles Blue. He threw the weapon on the ground and disappeared into the scene unfolding around him. A virtual vortex was created by the fleeing masses, leaving hundreds of bodies in it's wake.

John repeatedly tried to contact Fred Cook, but couldn't reach him on the 2-way radio.

"Okay fellas, we've got to get to the truck and get Donnie to the hospital. Chiefy isn't answering. Joel, you take the lead. I've got the back door. Can you stand up Donnie?"

"Yeah, I can do that. Let's just do this, man. I don't know how long I can last."

"If you have any problems, I'm *right behind you. We've got to get out of here now."*

Not being able to contact Fred left John feeling anxious about Robert's safety. The carnage that lay all around him was a stark reminder of the immeasurable consequences for such an ill-timed event of this magnitude to be played out in such an open environment. John shifted into survival mode and moved out.

****

Phillip Conover wrapped up the rifle and ran downstairs to the back door of the warehouse. He slowly cracked the door and peeped out. Suddenly, the door was kicked in, slamming into his face and knocking him to the floor.

"Damn, Silas. You done fucking busted my nose! What the hell are you doing here?"

"Just tying up some loose ends. Sorry Phil." Before Conover could move, Silas Bannister swung the shotgun into his face and squeezed the trigger. Phillip Conover died a very painful death.

"In here fellas! This guy has a rifle! We need a few more men to go inside and clear the building! Cal! dispatch and get an entry team here now!" The only link to the Sons of the New Confederacy had been eliminated.

****

Widespread looting fanned out away from the Monument Avenue District into the small and expensive shops that dotted the neighborhood. Law enforcement mostly stood back and allowed the mayhem to peter out. Most stayed together to avoid an ambush or mistaking a shopkeeper for a criminal. The National Guard and Virginia State Troopers eventually weaved into the turmoil and, after several hours, restored the immediate area in order to tend to the wounded and remove the dead. Thugs and opportunists vandalized and pilfered their way along the wide streets and headed towards downtown. Law enforcement scrambled to cut off streets to herd the masses towards the outer limits of the city. Tanks and armoured personnel vehicles were called in to force the crowds to disperse.

****

John Ashley and his team navigated the maze of protesters, cops and chaos to the Edgewood Avenue area where the car was parked. It was on fire. Again he tried to call Fred. No response. Donnie Musk was out of breath and strength. The loss of blood was slowly sapping his energy and John was beginning to struggle to keep him upright.

"Joel, if we don't get Donnie to a hospital soon, we're going to lose him. Keep your eyes open for Fred's ambulance. He should have been here by now. Anything you can find, get back here so we can get Donnie to a hospital. We'll wait here."

****

Fred Cook went to the back of the ambulance to retrieve bandages and antiseptics for the big gash to Robert Woods' forehead. He nervously scanned his surroundings for an accomplice. Satisfied that Rogers was acting alone, Fred wiped the blood from Robert's face and helped him to his feet.

"Fred ... what's going on?" Robert's head was pounding from the blow to his forehead.

"There's too much shit going on right now. I'll explain it to you later. Right now I have to get you to a doctor. I can't stop the bleeding."

"Where's John?"

"I don't know. The radio is busted so I can't get him. Now, enough talk. I'm gonna help you to the ambulance so I can get you some help. We've got to get out now!"

Robert stood and the carnage around him began to come into focus. Then he spotted Rogers' lifeless body lying only a few feet away.

"Damn! What happened to him?"

"The same thing that's going to happen to us if we don't get the fuck out of here fast, so I'm gonna help you to the ambulance.

Fred helped Robert into the front seat. He turned on the sirens and headed to Henrico Hospital downtown.

****

Edgar Caney weaved in and out of the alleyways, ducking behind cars and buildings whenever the police or armed scavengers appeared. Suddenly, a group of black youths that were trying to take advantage of the injured and dead by pilfering their money and valuables, eyed Edgar coming in their direction. Not satisfied with their present take, they turned their attention towards him.

Edgar turned around and walked briskly away, hoping against hope to simply get to safety. The recognizable patter of running feet towards him told him otherwise. They quickly overtook him when one of them threw a brick and struck him in the back of the neck. Edgar stumbled and tumbled to the ground. Six boys and young men pummeled him relentlessly, beating him unconscious.

"Stop! Stop now mother fuckers or you're dead!" It was the Level One Rapid Response Team assigned for extra security for the event. The offenders scrambled in different directions with several officers in pursuit. Edgar was out cold.

"Flag down that ambulance!" Sergeant Patterson stepped in front of Fred Cook, forcing him to slam on the brakes.

"I've got a seriously injured man here that needs medical attention. Open up the back so we can get him to a doctor."

Fred tried to protest, but his pleas fell to deaf ears. The unit loaded Edgar into the back and 2 of them stepped in.

"Ok, let's go!" Fred floored the pedal and continued on to the hospital. He didn't want to let them know that Robert Woods was riding up front because he didn't know who could be trusted. He was sure Robert had a concussion and might die if he didn't hurry.

****

The emergency room was teeming with activity as John, Donnie and Joel arrived at the hospital. A triage was set up in the parking lot to deal with the overwhelming amount of patients flooding in. Several doctors and nurses worked frantically to evaluate the incoming and assigned them according to the seriousness of their injuries. An untold number of dead were carted to the back of the parking lot for the coroners at a later time.

"Joel, help me get Donnie checked in at the front desk. Stay with him and make sure you don't leave him alone. We'll check him in as Robert Woods so he can get some immediate attention."

After making sure Donnie Musk was stabilized, John Ashley left to check the vast hospital for any sign of Fred or Robert. He peeped into every nook and cranny on the first floor, but couldn't find them. He then checked the emergency dock and peered into every arriving ambulance for any sign of the men. There was nothing.

John sat down on the curb and stared blankly at the scene unfolding all around him. Sleep crept in as he contemplated what to do next. Again he tried his radio. No answer.

****

Robert seemed to have a hundred questions about how he ended up in an ambulance and what all of the fuss was about. Fred cautiously obliged, making sure to keep his answers short and quiet so the men in the back couldn't hear.

"Robert, I want you to take it easy right now. That gash on your head looks pretty bad. We'll be at the hospital in a few minutes and as soon as a doctor has fixed you up, I'll get you up to date."

Robert began to feel dizzy and violently threw up on the dashboard. He blacked out and his breathing began to labor. Fred knew he had to reach a doctor quick.

****

Joel Macklin returned to the dock and found John Ashley asleep on his back. He gently nudged him awake.

"Here are a couple of sandwiches for you, John. They rushed Donnie to the second floor for surgery, but they kicked me out. They said there wasn't enough room for me to wait. I thought I might as well get us a bite to eat. I'm gonna hang out in the hallway until I can find out what his status is. He lost a lot of blood but they will post a guard at the door until he comes out. I think we both could use something to eat."

"Thanks Joel. I must have dosed off."

"Any word from Fred yet?"

"No. Not a thing. I'm getting kind of worried. Before you go back upstairs, check the main desk on the other side for any sign of Fred or Robert. Maybe they got caught up in the traffic or something. This can't be good."

"Right. And don't drift off too far away in case I find out something. This place is a nuthouse."

Just then, an ambulance screamed into the Sally Port with its lights blaring and stopped. It was Fred Cook. Robert was slumped down in the front seat and slipping in and out of consciousness. John sprang to his feet and opened the door. John caught him as he fell out.

"Fred, what happened?"

"We got stopped by Stacy Rogers on the way to the observation spot. He cracked him in the head with his gun pretty good just as he was coming out of his little nap. He must have followed us from the courthouse. 'Little Suzy' took care of that though. That arrogant son of a bitch was playing ball with the bad guys."

"Let's get him inside quick. He doesn't look good."

Joel grabbed Robert by his shoulders and Fred picked up his feet and rushed him into the hospital. John followed with his hand on his sidearm. He had come too far to lose him now.

John took the lead as the mass of injured and staff began to bog down in front of them.

"Nurse, we got a badly injured man here that needs help now! Can you help us?"

"We're full down here. Take him to the second floor to the Critical Care Unit. That's the best I can do.

John wanted to tell her that this was the 'real' Robert Woods, but he didn't think it would be a good idea. How could he explain that to the doctors, with Donnie Musk still in full makeup in emergency surgery already. He flashed his badge and the team rushed Robert to the elevator.

Meanwhile, Edgar Caney was whisked from the back of Fred's ambulance and through the emergency doors on a stretcher. His eyes were swollen shut, blood trickling from his mouth and nose, He too was barely clinging to life.

John Ashley suddenly remembered that he hadn't seen or heard from Charles Blue or any of the legal team that were on the reception stage. After getting Robert transferred to the medical staff, he headed back downstairs to check the registration desk for any word about his boss. A barrage of bullets had mowed down several people near him, so it hadn't crossed his mind that the others were probably struck.

As he neared the desk, he saw a familiar face. It was Ling Na Cho, Charles' Media Relations and Logistics representative for the team. She was bloodied and crying softly, leaning against a wall next to the women's bathroom.

"Ling! Are you alright?"

"Yes, thanks to Charles," she said. "When the shooting started, Charles grabbed me and wrapped his arms around me for protection, I guess. Then he was shot and we fell backwards off the stage. When the shooting died down, he was still on top of me, but he wasn't moving. That's when I saw he was shot and not breathing. He's dead John. I rode with him here and they put him out back with the rest of the dead until an autopsy can be done."

"What about you?"

"I'm alright. There was just so much blood. You know John, he saved my life. If it wasn't for him I would be dead too."

John wrapped his arms around her and she continued to cry. John could feel her body tremble slightly as he tried to comfort her. He didn't agree with Charles on a lot issues, but he did respect the fact that Charles spared no expense to see that Robert Woods and he got everything they needed to see the trial through. Danford Blue would have been proud of his son, he thought.

Ling finally calmed down and gathered her composure and wiped her face with a handkerchief.

"What about Mr. Woods? Is he here too?"

"Yeah. The doctors are looking him over now. I think he is going to be fine, but it's a little early to tell. Right now it looks like a concussion. We won't know anything until they check him out."

"Is anyone with him?"

"I've got a man with him. We just have to wait for the doctors to check him. He's got a pretty bad head wound."

****

The Critical Care Unit was flooded with activity; doctors, nurses and attendants scurrying about, trying to stabilize as many patients as possible. Robert Woods was rushed into a storage area that was converted into the initial treatment and diagnostic unit for trauma emergencies. There were 4 beds, separated by mobile curtains for privacy. Henrico Hospital is well equipped for the influx of patients, but even their preparation would be taxed in the coming days.

Ray Winslow, a freight truck driver from Raleigh, North Carolina, is in the bed closest to the nurses' station. He had been shot in the leg through the driver side door while waiting for the traffic to clear. Now he will be a guest for several more days.

In the second bed lay 'John Doe', better known as Edgar Caney. He had been scooped up in the fighting frenzy and deposited at the hospital with no identification and no money. A morphine drip helped ease the pain of a serious skull fracture and eyes swollen shut.

Next was Robert Woods. He is in a medically induced coma to help control the swelling brain that tinkered on the brink of erupting. John and his men had gotten him here just in time, but he was a long way from recovery. Joel Macklin was stationed at his bedside for protection. The last bed was empty, for now.

John Ashley followed the carnage taking over Richmond from the cafeteria's lounge television. News reports put the dead at several hundred and the injured and property damage was astronomical in its scope. He had no idea that the world wide reaction to the legislation in front of the Supreme Court would be so divisive.

National Guard Units upped the ante by using deadly force instead of negotiating with looters and any other criminal element. Mayor Jerry Armstrong declared a 'State of Emergency' and demanded the streets be cleared immediately for public safety. The newscast showed the people on the stage getting shot and the camera fell to the ground as everyone ran for their lives. John shook his head and headed back upstairs to check on Robert Woods and Donnie Musk. He first stopped to speak to Joel Macklin to get a progress report on Robert.

"What's up Joel? Any change?"

"Nothing yet. Blood pressure is good. The doctor or a nurse checks in pretty regular, so they say all we can do is wait. What about Donnie?"

"Heading there now. Stay here until one of us can relieve you. Don't let anybody back here that ain't supposed to be. Talk to you later."

****

The outside world came into focus as Edgar Caney came out of his medically induced stupor. He had another strange dream. This time it was about Robert Woods and how his newfound nemesis is 'doing much better'. His swollen eyes kept him from immediately recognizing his surroundings and his breathing was labored and painful. Just before sleep overtook him again, he couldn't make out the shadowy figures walking by the foot of his bed.

****

"Hey Fred, wake up!" It was John Ashley and the shift nurse checking on Robert Woods. Fred was jolted from his deep slumber and shot to his feet. He knocked his knife and sheath to the floor, but didn't notice.

"Sorry John. I guess I dozed off."

"Don't worry. No harm done. Joel I will be up here in a few minutes to relieve you. I can wait till he gets through with his dinner. I need you to go back to the motel and get some sleep yourself. We can get back to our families in a couple of days."

Fred groggily stood and left.

"So, what's the prognosis, ma'am? Is Mr. Woods going to be released any time soon?"

"I don't know. That will be up to Dr. Noble. As soon as the rest of his tests come back, I'm sure Doc will release him to your custody. I think it will be probably a couple more days."

"Well, I need to move him as soon as possible to a more secure location. You can see the toll this assignment has taken on my men. We all could use a little R and R."

Nurse Andrews said nothing, changing the bloody bandage on Robert's forehead. As she finished, Joel Macklin came in and watched as Nurse Brennan was finishing up.

"Ok Joel. The ball is in your hands. Fred will be here in the morning to relieve you. I'm going back downstairs to see how Donnie is doin'. See you in the morning."

John left and Nurse Brennan checked on her other patients in the room. Edgar was careful not to move as she checked his chart and scribbled down that he didn't appear to have regained consciousness. He stayed that way until she left the room.

Edgar couldn't believe it. Robert Woods had been delivered to him anyway. His eyes were still swollen shut, but he knew he had to move as soon as possible if he wanted to take his revenge. He tried to open his eyes, but the bright lights forced him to abandon it for now.

"I'll try it again later."

****

Forensic fingerprint analysts weaved in and out of the makeshift morgue in the parking lot at Henrico Hospital to expedite the identification process involving hundreds of bodies that were unclaimed by relatives or friends. The smell of decaying bodies began to overtake the surrounding neighborhoods even though local authorities had converged swiftly in response to the violence. After 3 days, hundreds of medical technicians and coroners from several states were dispersed throughout Richmond and other affected jurisdictions to hopefully avert a serious health crisis.

While talking to Donnie Musk, John Ashley watched intently as the wave of state and federal agents moved from room to room, sweeping up suspected antagonist and criminal suspects along the way. Suddenly, it dawned on him that Donnie Musk had been checked in under Robert Woods' name in order to get a quicker response for Donnie's shoulder wound. John was still mistrusting of anyone beyond the immediate security team. Stacy Rogers had sealed that.

"Donnie, I've got to move you out of here for a while. I'm gonna move you up to Robert's room. That way we can keep an eye on both of you at the same time. I can get you settled in up there and switch the charts after we get an update on Robert."

"Whatever you say John. I've got a few more days and I'm out."

John surveyed the hallway and started wheeling Donnie for the nearest elevator. He was fully geared up, sidearm and security badge in plain view. The transition went smooth and swift.

As John entered the Critical Care Unit, John began to feel dizzy and supported himself on Donnie's wheelchair. He tried to recover before anyone saw him, but it was too late.

Joel rushed over to hold John up.

"John! You okay?"

Up to now, John had been stoic in the face of all of the obstacles so far. The same problem that was beginning to plague the other members of the team, fatigue, had finally caught up to him. John was well aware how the effects of a non-rested prey can ultimately become fatal. He was battling an enormous amount of individuals and organizations whose sole purpose was to destroy them.

"Thanks Joel. I guess we all need a break. Put Donnie in the last bed. I'll try to rustle up a couple cups of coffee downstairs. I'll be right back.

Joel pushed Donnie to the back of the room, next to Robert Woods. Robert was still at least a couple of days away from being released, spending most of his time sleeping it off.

****

For several hours, Edgar Caney monitored the comings and goings of the hospital staff. He also used the wall clock to approximate the rounds made by the doctors and nurses to his area. He would have at least a 35 minute interval to get out. A dragnet of local and federal authorities were slowly tightening the noose around the hospital and Edgar knew time was running out.

A sterile bag next to his bed contained his clothes and shoes. After each nurse's rounds, Edgar climbed out of the bed and dressed himself, slipping back under the covers before anyone noticed. Even Joel Macklin bobbed and weaved in and out of sleep, oblivious to what was going on around him.

The measured whimpers of the monitors was soon interrupted by the subtle sound of Joel finally drifting off to 'Sleepland'. It was now or never for Edgar Caney. He shut off his monitor and removed the needle from his left arm. Edgar peeped towards the reception area and then to the back at his immediate surroundings. A shining object on the floor under Joel's chair caught his eye. As he creeped closer to get a better look, the object came into focus; a Huntsman knife in an ankle sheath in plain sight.

Edgar took a deep breath and again checked the front for any movement in his direction. There was none. He tiptoed towards the knife, never taking his eyes off of Joel, who was now completely sleep.

Edgar reached down and picked up the knife and sheath. Sweat began to bead on his forehead as the rush of his favorite killing tool back in his hands had returned the familiar tingle that surely meant death to all enemies. After removing the knife, he crept behind Joel and braced. Edgar dropped the sheath on

Joel's foot to get him to sit up. Joel sat up, only to feel the agonizing pain of the knife raking across his throat. He tried to scream, but no sound would come. Joel's body went limp, with Edgar holding on to lower him slowly to the bloody floor.

Edgar peered at the other two men in the back and suddenly realized that they looked almost identical. He had to move fast or it would surely be almost impossible to get out. On the chart next to the last bed, he found what he was looking for. It said "Robert Woods'.

"I got you now, mother fucker!"

Edgar raised the knife high into the air and.......blood sprayed everywhere.

It was over!

As soon as Edgar Caney plunged Fred Cook's knife into Donnie Musk's chest, alarms blared loudly from the monitor. Edgar briskly strolled to the exit as two nurses rushed into the room. He stuffed the bloody knife into the back of his pants and calmly walked towards the elevator.

"Blue Team, STAT, second floor, ICU, STAT!"

"Damn!" John Ashley immediately realized most of his team was in that area. He sprinted to the emergency elevator and forced his way inside. For what seemed like an eternity for him, the elevator doors opened up to a mass of humanity scrambling to resuscitate Joel Macklin and Donnie Musk.

John pushed his way in as best he could to the entrance of the Intensive Care Unit. He held up his credentials and was allowed to press forward to get a better look at the carnage.

"Sorry sir, you have to wait here! We've got 2 down and one missing. Wait in the hallway with security. We need to try to save these men.

A Virginia State trooper shuffled the gathering onlookers to the steps to make room for the doctors, nurses and equipment flooding to the floor from the elevator. John again flashed his badge to get the trooper's attention.

"Hey buddy, what's going on? I've got men in there and I need to know what's going on."

"Oh yeah? Well it ain't good. We got 2 stabbed and 1 missing. We are going over the security cameras now to find out what happened. As soon as I can clear this floor I'll see what I can do."

John weighed his options, but none seemed feasible. He tried to reach Fred Cook at his hotel room. No answer.

****

Edgar Caney had been ushered downstairs with the rest of the gawkers as John had stepped off of the elevator. He walked, still dazed from all of the intravenous medications injected during his brief stay. He shuffled down Broad Street towards the bright lights of downtown to try to put some distance between him and the carnage he had left behind at Henrico Hospital.

John Ashley was speechless when he got the news. Joel Macklin and Donnie Musk were dead. Robert Woods was dizzy, but coherent. Detectives and forensic investigators poured over the bloody scene.

"Robert, did you see anything?"

"Naw, John. I just heard a lot of commotion, machines going off and shit. Man! It seems like I'm fucking knocked out every time something happens."

"Can you walk? We need to get out of here."

John's eyes scanned the immediate area, watching for any sign of danger. He also knew that authorities would soon discover that Donnie Musk's true identity would be brought to light shortly. He had to get out now.

Dressed in his medical garbs, Robert Woods was supported by John to the Deputy Sheriff manned staircase for the trip to the first floor. He found an unoccupied wheelchair and gently lowered Robert down.

A hastily organized news conference sprang up in the lobby, with doctors, investigators, and different police agencies standing behind a bank of microphones.

Richmond police chief Jeoff Love stepped to the podium:

"This news conference is designed to get out important information to the public to capture a wanted fugitive that may be responsible for as many as eight murders in the state. His name is Edward Wayne Caney Jr., last known address is listed as 4912 Harris Rd., Henryville, Va. He has been sighted in this area and is believed to be injured but armed and dangerous."

Chief Love held up Edgar's Virginia driver's license photo and continued.

"If you see or make contact with the subject, do not approach. Contact law enforcement and stay clear. We will not take any questions now but will give you an update in about four hours."

Everyone quickly evacuated the area, but not before John got a glimpse of the knife the chief was carrying against his clipboard. It looked very familiar.

"Damn, that's Fred's knife!" He almost said it out loud.

As reporters yelled out questions that got no response, John wheeled Robert out of the hospital to find transportation to the Interstate 95 Motel where Fred Cook was sleeping.

****

Edgar Caney blended in among the hundreds of thousands of squatters, now homeless residents, and desperate citizens, left destitute over the last 48 hours. Local charities and churches assumed the enormous task of feeding and clothing stranded stragglers left dazed by the protests.

There were intermittent sweeps of the crowds to weed out trouble makers and felons. Ramped up police tactics began to effectively thin the hordes of hangers-on. State, federal, and local task forces eventually gained control of the streets.

Cities like Baltimore, Maryland, Washington, D.C., and Los Angeles, California struggled to maintain order. The cries of local politicians and law enforcement were largely ignored. For the first time in recent history, the Pentagon is enlisted by the federal government to restore order.

****

Fred Cook woke up both groggy and hungry. The television was low, but barely audible. Through blurred vision, Fred made out the picture of the screen. It was a picture of Robert Woods. He lunged for the remote to listen.

"... Breaking News! Plaintiff Robert Woods has been found stabbed to death in his hospital room by hospital staff responding to an internal alert. Mr. Woods, along with at least one member of his security team was killed at Henrico Hospital."

"Investigators have determined the fatal wounds were inflicted by this car large combat knife that was reportedly found at the scene. One patient was also reported missing. WRCH will continue to update you as we get more information. Reporting live from downtown Richmond, Terry Abrams, Action News 10."

"Chiefy" was incredulous to what he just saw. He tossed his clothes, patted his legs and scanned the room.

It was his knife!

Fred sat down slowly on the bed and contemplated his options. The very man he was assigned to protect was not only dead but he would be held responsible. His phone flashed briskly from the several messages he had already missed.

****

John Ashley and Robert woods stepped out of the Army Rescue Jeep and headed into the lobby of the Interstate 95 Motel in North Richmond. They boarded the elevator and headed for the eighth floor. Again, John is greeted by a swarm of police and crime scene tape blocking the hallways.

****

"Hey! What's going on here? I need to get to my room!"

"Sorry. This floor is shut down. Didn't somebody tell you in the lobby?"

"No. I'm John Ashley. Head of Security for the floor." John flashes his security pass, but didn't press.

"Let me get the captain for you. What rooms did you have?"

"874 and 876."

"Yeah. Wait right here for a sec. I'll be right back."

"Robert, I don't like the looks of this. Whatever happens, you gotta stay close to me. Got that?"

"Gotcha John. Man, I hope Chiefy is O.K."

"Hey, you! Captain wants to talk to you. Come on down."

John walked down to room 874 with Robert in tow. He was stopped in the doorway.

Keland Harris, an ex-Division II football player completely blocked the entrance with his massive 6' 6", 280 lb. frame.

"Which one of you is John Ashley?"

"I am!"

"You can step inside but don't touch anything." The officer held out his arm as Robert approached.

"Who are you?"

"Well, my name Is ..."

John Ashley broke in, he didn't want to expose Robert until he knew what was going on.

"He's with me. Part of my security crew. He's O.K."

"He stays here. You, come with me."

John scanned the room, with no sign of Fred Cook. The television was on the news channel with the continuous loop of the Henrico Hospital news conference blaring in the background.

****

Pictures of Robert Woods were plastered everywhere as crowds around the country began to swell. Thousands of protesters descended on Monument Avenue to destroy a considerable number of Confederate statues to avenge the murders. State troopers held the crowds at bay.

At least for now.

Captain Harris led John cautiously around the foot of the bed. First feet then legs and finally a large figure lay on the floor with a towel over his face, blood soaking through,

Captain Harris raised the towel to expose the gruesome site of Fred Cook's stiff body with a gaping hole in the side of his head. His trusty armpit .25 automatic laying nearby.

"You know this guy?"

John was stunned. He and Fred grew up together on the rough streets of Northwest Baltimore. Now his best friend was gone.

"Yeah. He's one of my men. Fred Cook, I know his wife and family. What happened?"

"Looks like he shot himself or someone wants it to look like it. Security responded pretty quickly when the shot was fired. No one entered or left the room. We already viewed the security tape. Any idea why he would do this to himself, John?"

John didn't respond. He stared at the knife, still shown at the news conference and reasoned in a matter of little time, the police and investigation would figure out the knife belonged to Chiefy. John just couldn't figure out how it ended up in Donnie Musk at Henrico Hospital.

John quickly realized that Robert was staring at the television in amazement at the carnage erupting around him. John quickly grabbed Robert's arm and headed down the hallway.

"Captain, we've got to get back to the hospital as soon as possible. I've got some other men that have to be contacted." Robert tried to process what he just seen, but John shoveled him out of hearing distance.

"Robert, there's a lot going on the last 24 hours and I don't have time to explain it to you now. If we don't get out of here, we could be next. Don't say anything, just move."

RICHMOND, VIRGINIA

The Boat

(6 months later)

Richmond, Virginia

Robert Woods and John Ashley stood on the Shockoe Bottoms loading docks waiting to board the luxurious yacht, "Annie Mae" for the ceremonial repatriation voyage to Monrovia, Liberia.

The boat will be escorted by several local, state, and federal vessels down the James River to Virginia Beach. A refurbished cargo ship stood at the ready for the 6-day cruise.

"Good luck to you Robert, stay safe. For a long stretch, I didn't think neither of us would be here."

"Yeah, I know, John. We lost a lot of good people along the way. But we are not the first to do this. We are only the "NEXT." I want to be there while I can still make a contribution. No More Excuses."

A long, steady blow of the vessel's horn signaled for all aboard. John Ashley was never a guy that showed much emotion and it wasn't going to be observed here, but his stomach did seem to boil with pride as he watched Robert ascend the gang-plank and melt into the bowels of the spacious yacht.

As the Flotilla slowly navigated the James River, Robert reflected on the adventure and unknown that was to come. There was a brief flicker of what was to remain behind but steeled himself to the new that lies ahead.

Monrovia, Liberia

Goodbye, Robert Woods! Find the peace and understanding you richly deserve.

Conspiracy Theories

#1 – A Democratic President, Andrew Johnson, rescinded the "40 Acres and a Mule" promised to freed slaves after the Civil War, the first reversal of reparations. Johnson became president of the United States after the assassination of President Abraham Lincoln, a Republican.

#2 – The state of Georgia is responsible for more lynchings than any other state.

#3 – U.S. Government operatives assigned to destroy and decimate the Black population through the experimentation of infections using syphilis, birth control, starvation, and "any means necessary."

#4 – The Central Intelligence Agency introduced crack cocaine into several Los Angeles neighborhoods to finance an illegal war in Central America and at the same time destabilize the Black community. To this date, crack cocaine has been the CIA's most successful immobilization and extermination program in the agency's history. As a result, the president's "War on Drugs," has incarcerated hundreds of thousands all over the country. Federal, state, and local coffers have enriched their budgets through imprisonment, confiscation of property, and death. Local police departments allow open- air drug markets, murders, and judicial misconduct that proliferates even today.

#5 – They don't call it the "White House" because of the color of the paint, but for the racial superiority of their ancestors.

#6 – Politicians raise and spend millions of dollars to earn a job that pays thousands. Infer what you want. It just doesn't make any sense.

#7 – If there is a "separation of church and state" why are pastors and other religious figures allowed to run for state office?

#8 - Religious leaders on the "Trinity Broadcasting Network" recently proposes making the city of Jerusalem the capital of the world. Why?

#9 - Italian leader, Benito Mussolini, during World War 2 stated Black people don't deserve a history and Italian disdain exists even today through popular television programs such as "The Sopranos."

www.ingramcontent.com/pod-product-compliance
Ingram Content Group UK Ltd.
Pitfield, Milton Keynes, MK11 3LW, UK
UKHW020700200225
455358UK00010B/514

9 798822 934313